THE DARK SIDE OF SECRETS

A Madison Hart Mystery

DB JONES

Chapter One

IT WAS A SMOLDERING SUMMER, AND MADISON HART and her partner, Detective Josh Logan, of the Maitland Police Department had just finished one of the most bizarre cases they had ever encountered. It took them down some of the most twisted and complex trails of possession, revenge, greed and murder. Madison had spent most of her career as a Criminal Investigator and Profiler for the FBI. But, after years of living out of her suitcase and flying all over the country, she returned to her hometown of Maitland, Florida, and opened a Private Investigation Agency.

After wrapping up the case, she spent some time in Cassadaga, Florida, with her sister, Winter Hart, to decompress. The case still haunted her, but being with her sister and strolling through the streets of this quiet little town she felt balanced again and ready to go back to work.

The agency was on one side of a duplex located about a five-minute walk from the townhouse she was renting. She was anxious to see what would land on her desk next. She packed up her things, said her goodbye to her sister, and put her little dog, Sophie, into her car seat and headed for home.

Driving past the old Cassadaga Hotel brought back good times of sitting out on the massive wrap-around porch and having coffee or tea while watching the tourists gather for a tarot card or psychic reading from one of the residents. Cassadaga was touted as the spiritual capital of the world and shingles swung from the quaint homes that dotted the narrow street.

She remembered feeling the sweet morning breezes as they brushed the bougainvillea vine that cascaded over the trellis at the end of the hotel's porch. She loved visiting there, but home was home, and work was what she needed.

She hadn't seen or heard from Josh in a couple of weeks, and that was a bit disturbing. During their entire case, they had been attached at the hip and to go cold turkey without him for a few weeks was uncomfortable for her.

Madison left the town limits and entered the on-ramp of Interstate -4 and drove west. She saw the Maitland interchange in the distant; she was almost home. She turned onto Maitland Avenue until she hit Horatio which was the main street through town. Coming down Maitland Avenue always felt good as she was driving down the same road she rode her bicycle on as a young girl. But coming up on the Maitland Police Department got her heart racing. Would Josh be glad to see her? Would there be another case? Suddenly, doubt riddled her short-lived tranquility. Uncertainty flooded her thoughts, something she rarely felt as a Criminalist Investigator. Her car wanted to turn into the Police station parking lot the same way it had done the past year; but she needed to get home, unpack and let Sophie out. She turned onto Swoope Avenue and slowly drove past the front of her office. She could have sworn she saw someone walking around inside, but it must have been the shadows of the swaying trees.

She would be on her own for the first time since she took a leave of absence from the FBI. They allowed her on an extended leave of absence that gave her a backdoor if her agency failed. So far the only cases she got were those from her friend, Jim Tucker, of the Orlando Sentinel. Although they were amazing, complicated cases, she was ready to generate a case on her merits as a P.I.

She pulled into her driveway and noticed there was something sitting at the front door. She let Sophie out and slowly walked to the door not knowing what to expect. There was a basket of cheeses, a bottle of wine, and a large bar of dark chocolate. She hesitated for a moment. The last time there was something at her door, it was from a stalker from a previous case. However, it couldn't be from him; he was killed by his insane lover. "This is not something Josh would do, or at least he never had before, and besides, how would he know I was coming home today?" There was a card tucked in the basket. Sophie was jumping at the front door, so she unlocked the door, carried the basket in and set in on the kitchen counter and then opened the French doors to her patio for Sophie.

Madison plopped down on the couch and opened the card.

"Welcome home partner, Enjoy."

She crinkled her nose and tilted her head. "How did he know I would be arriving today?" Her heart started to beat faster at the thought that this might be from Josh.

Knock, Knock

Sophie ran in from the patio and dashed past Madison to the door, sniffed the threshold and started wagging her tail. She turned to Madison and started spinning in circles; there was no guessing who it could be. She only acted that way for one person...Josh.

Knock, Knock.

"Who is it?" she teased.

"It's the cops, open the door or we'll bust it down."

Madison opened the door, and Sophie squeezed her head between the door and the wall and started her excited little bark she does when she is happy to see someone. Josh reached down and picked her up. "Good to see you, too." Sophie planted a big lick across his face. "That's the best kiss I've had in a long time."

Madison stood against the door as he entered carrying Sophie. "Come in."

He put the pup down on the couch and walked over to the basket of goodies. He lifted one eyebrow. "Hmmm, another secret stalker?"

Her eyes widened, she stepped back from the basket as though it was about to explode and tossed the card on the table, "I thought this was from you?"

Josh couldn't hold back his laughter. "I'm just jerking your chain. Yeah, I brought them over to welcome you back home."

She slapped him on the arm. He drew up, anticipating another slug from her, but she reached over, grabbed him, and planted a big kiss on his lips.

"That's the second best kiss I've had in a long time," he chuckled.

"Well, it just might be your last," she snickered. "How did you know I was coming home today?"

"I have my sources. I am an ace detective you know."

"Did my sister call and tell you?"

He glanced to the side and down, raised his eyebrows and tightened his lips. "No, she did not call me."

"You are such a liar."

"No, she didn't call *me*, I called her to see how you were doing. I've got to know my partner is okay, right? And you're welcome."

"Huh…Oh, thank you for the gift."

"Okay lady, I'm going to get out of your hair so you can get settled. I have a meeting with the chief in the morning, but I'll swing by your office later. Welcome home, I've missed you."

"Thank you, Josh." She wanted to tell him she missed him too but didn't. "I'll be in the office early. I want to touch base with Becca and see if we've had any calls. I guess I'm on my own now. I have to admit that it's a bit unnerving not knowing where my next case is coming from, or *if* there is going to be another one."

"I'm sure your phone will be ringing off the hook with cases, don't worry. I'll see you tomorrow."

She walked him to the door, gave him a peck on the cheek and watched him walk out. He honked the horn and waved as he drove off. She walked out to the backyard to check on Sophie and saw her neighbor and assistant, Becca Hamilton, standing there with her glass of wine. "Welcome back," Becca called out.

"Thanks, it's good to be home. I was going to call you later to see if you were ready to go to work in the morning."

"I'm ready. I was getting bored sitting around the house all day. I have been checking the calls each day, but nothing has come in. There were a few prank calls from kids; but nothing that warranted calling anyone back. Would you like a glass of wine?" Becca asked.

"Sure, that would be nice. Let me unload the car first. Why don't you come over in about fifteen minutes?"

"Do you need any help unloading?

"Not really. Most of it is Sophie's stuff. I can't believe a little dog needs so much when we travel. I think I packed more for her than I did for me," Madison chuckled.

As she unloaded the car, the realization hit hard that she would have to generate cases if her agency was going to make a go of it. That was something she never had to think about while working with the FBI; there was always a case to be investigated and a mystery to be solved. So far, the only cases she had were from Jim Tucker in conjunction with the Maitland Police Department.

Madison had taken off for two weeks after the last case but was ready to start her business. There was the possibility of relocating to the FBI office in the area, but she was determined to give a chance to her dreams of becoming an independent P.I.

Becca came in through the back gate of Madison's courtyard.

She was not only her assistant but her neighbor and the daughter of Madison's mother's best friend. Becca had also grown up in Maitland and knew many of the same people Madison knew, and she was very familiar with the area. That came in handy when Madison needed an extra hand.

"How was your time off with your sister Winter?"

Madison poured two glasses of wine and sunk into the overstuffed chair in the living room. She took a deep breath and sighed. "I can understand why Winter loves living there. Every time I drive into that little town, my whole body starts to relax. I'm not sure if it's just knowing that I'm there to unwind with my sister or the gentle pace of everyone that lives there. Either one, I enjoy hanging out with my sister. But I must admit the last few days I started getting antsy about work."

"Have you heard from Detective Logan since you've been back?"

"As a matter-of-fact, he had a gift basket waiting for me, and he stopped by for a short visit. He said he would see me in the morning. I think he'll be swinging by the office early before he heads to the station," Madison replied.

Becca smiled. "I think he misses the challenge of the cases too, and I know he missed you."

"What makes you say that?"

Becca tilted her head, raised one eyebrow, and gave one of those enigmatic smiles. "Seriously? Girl, are you blind?"

Madison just took another sip of her wine and smiled.

They reflected on the last case, how bizarre it was and how complex the characters were. Madison admitted that was one mystery that still has her head spinning.

Becca finished her wine and started for the back gate. "Well, I'd better get going and let you settle in. I'll see you in the morning." Madison walked her to the gate and stood while Sophie did her business in the backyard, then went back inside and shut the French doors. She poured another glass of wine and headed for bed. She wanted to get to the office early the next day and box up everything from the last case. She was eager to set-up the command room so it would be ready for the next caseload, assuming there was going to be another one.

Chapter Two

The morning seemed to come quickly on her first day back to town. Sophie curled up against Madison trying to get under the covers. The rain was beating hard against the French doors that led out to the patio. It sounded like pellets of rocks hammering at it. Madison lifted the covers just enough for the little pup to squeeze in. Her little body was shaking. "It's okay, girl, it's just the rain," Madison said stroking Sophie, trying to calm her. She glanced at the clock. "Oh crap, it's 8:30 a.m.," she hollered as she jumped out of bed. Sophie remained under the covers as Madison quickly showered and dressed in a long teal button-down blouse and tight-fitting black leggings. "I wanted to be at the office before now. Come on girl, let's go outside."

Sophie crawled out from the covers and ran towards the patio, however, when Madison opened the door just enough for Sophie to go outside, she sat down, turned and looked up at Madison. The rain was coming in the door, and thunder was clamoring away outside. "Okay, you can use the potty pad today." She closed the door, grabbed her briefcase and darted for her car.

She reached for the car door expecting to leap into the seat, but the door wouldn't budge. The battery in her keyless entry wasn't working. She scrambled through her purse trying to find the key. She struggled to get the manual key out of the keyless device. Her wet hair was dripping on her shoulders and down the front of her blouse. She finally got the door opened and jumped in, but it was too late, her clothes were sopping wet. She banged her fist on the dashboard. "Damn, this is not how I wanted to begin my first day back."

She jerked the car door open and dashed for the front door of her place. When she opened the door, Sophie greeted her as though she had been gone all day, but Madison wasn't in the mood for niceties. She dropped her wet clothes onto the bathroom floor, rubbed the towel through her hair, changed and grabbed her umbrella, and raced back to the car.

As she pulled up to the office, she saw Josh's car parked out front. Fortunately, Josh left her enough room to park near the entrance. She popped open the umbrella and darted for the door. Just as she reached for the doorknob, Josh swung it open. "Good morning," he smiled.

Madison lowered her head and gave him a look that would kill. "Well, it hasn't started out that way," she grumbled.

"Oh, I see you washed your hair."

She slightly tilted her head to one side and dropped her chin while looking at him. "No, I was stuck in the rain."

Josh quickly diverted the conversation. "I brought coffee and bagels."

Becca walked out from the back room with her coffee. "Good morning, Boss."

Josh stood behind Madison, and glanced over at Becca and shook his head motioning that it wasn't a good morning for Madison.

"Good morning to you too," Madison replied. "Any calls?"

Becca swallowed the gulp of coffee she was sipping, "No, not yet, but it's early."

Josh rolled his eyes and reached for the bag of bagels. "How was your visit with Winter?"

"It was great. I sure can see why she loves living there. I think I might retire there."

"You can't leave," Josh blurted out.

"I didn't say I was going to move there tomorrow. I meant it was a quiet and laid-back place."

"Any new cases in the major crime unit, Josh?"

"It's been pretty quiet there too. The only calls the department has had since you left were a few domestic disputes and a break-in at the one of the warehouses. The chief likes it that way. But to tell you the truth, it's boring and I miss the challenge."

Madison slowly walked to the back room. Josh followed, but Becca stayed at the front desk. He closed the door behind him and stood to look at the whiteboard. "It seems odd not having the board filled with information, doesn't it?"

Madison stood there silently staring at the board and then turned to him. "Josh, have I made a mistake leaving the bureau? I can't depend on Jim Tucker to keep my business running. I wonder if all this is just a pipe-dream."

He stepped up close to her, put his hand on her shoulders and lifted her chin. He softly smiled. "Ms. Hart, look at me. You're a damn good investigator. You might not have the phone ringing off the hook with potential cases yet, but give it time."

"I guess I was expecting to come back from Winter's and have to decide which one to choose. I was fooling myself into believing this would work. I can always ask Stratton to reassign me to the local FBI division, but damn, Josh, I want this to work."

"Come on Hart, grab one of those bagels, clean off the board and sip your coffee. That crazy case that you seem to attract so well is on its way."

She reached up and kissed him, then sipped her coffee. "Why didn't you bring donuts?"

"Woman, you drive me nuts."

She opened the door and headed back to the reception area. Just as she was about to ask Becca if she would get some donuts, the phone rang.

Madison held her breath as Becca answered the phone, "Hart Agency." That was all she said. She was doing all the listening, and then, "One moment please, Ms. Hart is with a client. Let me see if she can talk to you." Becca put the call on hold. She dropped her shoulders, took a long, deep breath and looked up at Madison. "Ms. Hart, you have a call. You might want to take this in your office."

Madison hurried to her office, sat down behind her desk, and tried to catch her breath before picking up the receiver.

She counted, one…two…three…four…five, and then answered the phone. "Madison Hart,"

Josh remained in the front with Becca. "Okay, what was that about?" he whispered.

Becca scrunched her shoulders and clasped her hands as though in prayer. She grinned so big that the light from the lamp reflected on her teeth. "Hopefully a case," she said trying not to hollered it out.

Josh tilted his head back and let out the air he was holding in.

Madison was in her office for nearly an hour. Becca was nervous, but it didn't compare to what Josh was feeling. He was pacing the room like an expectant father, and the perspiration was dripping off his forehead. "Good grief, how long is she going to be in there?"

Suddenly they heard Madison's office door open. She slowly walked to the front with her head slightly bowed. When he saw the way she looked, a knot formed in the pit of his stomach. He was afraid to ask, but couldn't stand the suspense. "Well?"

She hesitated for a moment looked over at Becca and then back at Josh, "WE HAVE A CASE!" she screamed. Becca dropped her head on the desk in relief. Josh grabbed Madison and swung her around. "I knew it. I knew it. You're like a friggin crime magnet," he snickered.

"What's *our*, I mean your case?" he asked.

"Just a minute, I can't breathe. I need to sit down. Why don't we all go into the other back room," she mumbled. "It's not a big case, but it's a start and she wants me to investigate."

Becca and Josh took a seat as Madison stepped up to the board. She picked up the dry-erase marker and wrote down the first word *Missing*, and then wrote **Zoe McClain**.

"It's a missing person's case. The woman who just called was the mother. She has been calling her daughter for over a week with no luck. She told me that her daughter recently moved into a shared apartment to cut down on her expenses. She just got the teaching position she'd been hoping for, so the mother assumed it was taking much of her daughter's time. But when she didn't call over the weekend, she started to worry. Her daughter never missed calling her on Sunday, and this was the second Sunday she missed calling. The mother stopped by her daughter's apartment, and the roommate escorted her to Zoe's room, but when she entered her daughter's room, it was empty. Apparently, she just left without saying a word to the roommate or her mother. The mother admitted her daughter had done this before when she wasn't satisfied with the living conditions. So, her mother wants me to find where her daughter moved to," Madison added.

"I know you, and I suspect there is something churning in that mind of yours. What is your gut telling you?" Josh asked.

Madison jotted down a few things on the board under the name of the missing girl, Zoe. "Okay, here's what I know so far, which is very little: Zoe shared an apartment with Jon Smith."

"Jon Smith? Is that for real?" Becca asked with a chuckle.

"Yes, it's Jon Smith."

"Jon Smith was the roommate. When he came home after the weekend with his girlfriend, he noticed Zoe had moved out. She stripped her room clean and even took the furniture. The roommate was upset because it left him paying everything," Madison continued.

"Did she take her car?" Becca asked.

"I suppose so, it's not at her apartment. I'll start with interviewing the roommate."

Josh finished his coffee and bagel and started out the door. "Where are you going?" Madison asked.

"I have to go to work," he groaned.

"Okay, I'll talk to you later."

Madison stood staring at the board the way the two of them had done on the last two case together, but this was her case, and she didn't need his help this time. His demeanor shifted; his shoulders drooped, and he slowly walked out the door. The rain had stopped. He slowly got into his car and started the car. He began to back out of the driveway when Madison began pounding on his window. It startled him and as he whipped around he saw her nose was nearly pressed up against the glass.

"Yeah, what is it?" he asked, as he let down the window.

"You were right, thank you."

"I knew a case would show up for *you* soon."

"Josh, I know you can't officially work with me, but I might need you," she smiled.

"Just say the word. Now get off of my car so I can earn my salary."

He wanted to jump out of the car and smother her with kisses. *She might need me.* He honked the horn and drove off.

By the time Madison returned to the case room, Becca had reorganized the board more clearly, beginning with a timeline of the last time the mother had spoken to her daughter. Madison stood there with her hands on her hips, smiling as she shook her head. "Becca, you just might have to start studying for your P.I. license. You certainly have a head for this.

"It's so similar to the way I set up the board when I worked for the attorney. It's a plot board, so the details follow a sequential pattern leading up to the resolution. It gives you a better visual of the case."

"I sure could have used you when I was with the FBI, but then they would have taken you from me," she chuckled. "Oh, and thanks for boxing up the old case. I see you have it all labeled too, thanks."

"Just doing what you pay me to do," Becca smiled.

"I'm going over to talk to the roommate and check out the room. Would you mind asking the mother to file a formal missing person's report on her daughter. We want this to go into the National Law Enforcement Database as soon as possible, and don't forget to remind her to include her daughter's date of birth," Madison urged.

Chapter Three

Madison drove over to Zoe's apartment. The shared apartment was on the back side of the apartment complex on the bottom floor. There were a few neighbors outside with their children, so she stopped and asked if anyone knew Zoe but drew a blank. She checked with some of the other neighbors to see if any of them had seen or talked to Zoe lately. No one in the complex had met her yet, but a few had seen her coming and going on occasion. They said the roommate had lived there for awhile and was surprised to see a young woman move in since he had a girlfriend who was there frequently.

Next step was to interview the roommate, Jon Smith. Every time she said the name, she almost laughed. *Jon Smith? He wouldn't make that up.* She knocked on the door, and a tall, lanky good looking young man answered the door.

"Jon Smith?"

"Yes, and you must be Ms. Hart? Please come in." He appeared to be an easy going man and was soft spoken.

The place was neat with a comfortable décor. It certainly didn't look like a bachelor's pad, and she wondered if his girlfriend had a hand in the decorating. "Nice place you have."

"Thank you, but I can't take the credit, Ginny picked out most of the furniture and decorated it for me. I'm not much into that sort of thing."

"Have you lived here long?"

"About a year and a half," he answered.

"How did you meet Zoe?"

"I put an ad in the paper for a roommate and she answered the ad."

"I've got to ask you, how did your girlfriend feel about you having a young woman as a roommate?"

"To tell you the truth, she wanted to meet her first, but after she had met Zoe, she was on board with the idea. I had been having trouble meeting my bills and started falling behind so I needed a roommate, and I figured a woman would help keep the place neat. I would feel more comfortable bringing Ginny here with a woman around, then having a guy living here and checking her out every time she came over. Besides, Zoe was easy going and reliable. She always paid me on time."

"Did you two get along well?" Madison carefully asked.

"If you mean, were we lovers? Hell no. I barely knew her. She kept to herself in her room most of the time."

"When was the last time you talked to Zoe?"

"She was heading off to her job one morning, I think it was Wednesday, and I briefly spoke to her just to tell her I was going away for the weekend. When I was getting ready to leave Friday evening her door was shut, so I just left. I didn't get back from Ginny's until late Sunday night, and her door was still closed."

"Do you mind if I have a look at her room?"

"No, not at all, but there isn't anything there. She moved out everything she had."

Madison opened the door to a stark room. There was nothing left in the room, not even a picture on the wall. She had stripped the room of any evidence of her ever being there. *She had to have help moving. A young, small frame woman wouldn't be able to carry out all the furniture on her own.* She left the room wondering if any of the neighbors had seen a truck over that weekend that Zoe went missing.

"Thank you so much for your help. If you can think of anything else, please give me a call," Madison stated as she handed him her card.

He calmly took the card and walked her to the door. "I sure hope she's alright. I know her mother is worried about her."

Madison nodded her head and left. She stood out front of the apartment glancing up and down the street and parking area. There was a guy coming out of his apartment about two doors down. She approached him and introduced herself. "Did you know the woman that lived in that apartment?" she asked pointing to the apartment.

"No, but then I haven't lived here long," he replied.

"Were you here this past weekend?"

"Yes."

"Did you notice a moving van or large truck moving anything out of that apartment?"

"No, and I think I would have noticed that because I was working on my car most of the day on Saturday and Sunday I had a few friends over, and we watched the game. But if a moving van were there, they'd have to pass my place to turn around."

Madison handed him her card, thanked him and left. She drove up to the turnaround at the end of the street to get a feel for what a truck would do. It would be difficult for a big moving van to make that turn, but a smaller van or pickup truck could easily make it. It was getting late in the day so she decided she'd come back on the weekend to talk to some of the other neighbors.

She climbed into her silver Prius and headed back to the office. The windows were up and the A/C was on full blast. She was investigating her first case on her own as a P.I., and it suddenly hit her. "Hot Damn, I'm a real P.I. with my own agency!" she yelled at the top of her lungs. "I am going to make this work."

Becca was still at the office when she returned. "Hey, what are you still doing here? It's after 5:00 p.m. It's not like we're in the heat of the case yet. I have a few things I want to do before I leave, so I'll see you tomorrow."

"Okay Boss, I'll see you in the morning. Becca grabbed her purse out of the bottom drawer of her the large oak desk and left.

Madison headed for the back room to jot down some information on the board. After the last case, she wondered if she would ever get all the marks off of it. The board had been slathered with clues and information, but erased and redone so many times due to the complex nature of the case that she was afraid the marks would be permanent. Becca had cleaned the board to look like new. Madison was so glad to have Becca working for her. She was perfect. Not only was Becca the daughter of Madison's mother's best friend, but she had a background in criminal cases when she worked for a defense attorney. Becca was her right-hand and made sure everything ran smoothly. Therefore, the board had always reflected the most up-to-date information. Madison no longer had to rummage through piles of papers trying to decipher what was what in a case.

She finished updating the board and was eager to get home. Sophie needed to be let out, and she wanted to finish settling back in after her trip. The excitement of a new case had her blood rushing. Though it was a simple missing person's case, it was a case.

Sophie greeted her at the door with her usual spinning in circles and then racing to the French doors to be let out. Madison was ready to call it a day. She wanted to slip into a hot bubble bath. She lit lavender scented candles throughout the house and turned on some relaxing flute music and was just about to slide into the tub when her cell phone rang. It was Josh.

"Hey, how did your first day on the job go?"

"Not too bad. I was able to see Zoe's room and talk to the roommate. I didn't learn much, except that he hadn't seen Zoe for nearly a week because he was staying with his girlfriend a lot."

"What are you doing now?" Josh cautiously asked.

"I'm just about to slip into my tub."

"You want any company?" he chuckled.

"Not tonight, but I'll take a raincheck on that," she sighed.

"I'm going to hold you to that. Just one more thing, and I'll let you go. Are you going to check with the girlfriend? Never mind, of course, you are."

"Don't you have any cases to work on?" she asked.

Josh hesitated. He didn't want to sound bored or eager to interject himself into her case, but he did miss working with her. "Yeah, I've got lots of cases," he boasted as he shuffled through a few papers. "Maybe, I'll swing by your office after work tomorrow and see how your new case is going. How about grabbing a bite to eat. The food trucks will be set up around Lake Lily tomorrow and you can fill me in. How does that sound?"

"Sounds great. We'll touch base then. Have a nice night," she whispered as she hung up.

Madison turned the lights off in the bathroom and slid into her bubble bath. Only the flicker of the candles lit the room. The flute music in the background was calming. She took of sip of Merlot wine and observed the sensation as it slid down her throat. She was feeling good about everything, her townhouse, her little companion, Sophie, Josh, and now she had a case. She could leave her office each day and come home to relax, something she didn't have while working with the FBI…or so she thought.

She hadn't been in the tub ten minutes when her cell phone rang. She started to reach for it and changed her mind. "No, whatever it is, it can wait. I am going to enjoy my relaxation." Madison lingered in the soothing waters for awhile and then finally got out and slipped on a pair of yoga pants, a fleece lined hoody and her pink fuzzy slippers. She was in for the night, and it felt good.

She checked her messages, and there was one from Josh. She hesitated to read it, but that old got-to-know instinct clicked in.

I was just thinking about the girlfriend. I can't imagine that having her man living with a young, well-built, attractive woman is going to set well with her, no matter what she told Smith. Sleep well and I'll talk to you tomorrow.

That thought had crossed her mind, but the roommate sounded so positive that his lady friend didn't mind. The more she thought about it, the more it bothered her. "Damn, just one night on a case I would like to come home and leave my work at the office, but I don't see that happening," she mumbled.

She stared at her cell as if it would tell her what to do next. "Oh Well." She clicked on Josh's icon. "Detective Logan at your service," he laughed.

"Okay, you might be right. Why don't you grab some Chinese take-out and come over? You can tell me what's really on your mind," she snickered.

"Thought you were going to bed or is that why you want me?" he joked.

"Just get over here," she demanded as she hung up the phone.

Josh was there within twenty minutes with enough food for ten people. He spread it out on the counter and handed her some chopsticks. "I couldn't remember which was your favorite," he grinned as he reached for the box with the Bar-B-Q Spare Ribs.

Madison just watched as he made himself at home. Inside she was smiling at his comfort around her. With her hands on her hips and tapping her foot, she protested a little anyway, "Why don't you just make yourself at home?" She looked over at him munching away on the ribs. "How do you know, that's not what I wanted to eat?"

He swallowed a big mouth full of meat and nearly choked. "You never eat the ribs."

She just laughed. "You think you know me so well, don't you? I just let you think I didn't like them."

He handed her the remaining box of ribs. "Here, there's plenty for both of us."

"Nah, I changed my mind, I don't want any tonight. I'll just have some Chicken Lo Mein," she said reaching for the box on the counter.

"Are you messing with me…again?"

She smiled. "It's just too easy to resist."

"Only with you because you're such a damn good interrogator. I'll bet you have the suspects confess to crimes they know nothing about, just out of fear."

"Do I really come across as being such a hard-ass?"

"Got ya," he laughed.

She reached over and slapped his arm. "Yes, you did."

"This reminds me of the fun we had working together on the last two cases," he grinned as he scraped the meat off of the rib.

"Fun? I wouldn't exactly call it fun when someone tried to kill me," she grumbled.

"Well, that was not what I meant. I was referring to the part about you and me working together."

She glanced at him and burst out laughing. He had Bar-B-Q sauce all over his chin and down the sides of his mouth.

"What?"

She bit her lower lip to keep from laughing any harder. "Got to love a man who gets into his food."

All Josh heard were the words, got to love a man. Nothing else mattered at that moment.

She couldn't wipe the smile off of her face while she was trying to eat.

"You find this funny, do you?" he asked as he grabbed her and planted a big kiss on her mouth. She started to pull away, but when he backed up she pulled him to her, with the sauce and all and returned his kiss. Josh set the box of ribs on the counter, and she placed her box of Lo Mein down too. He backed her into her bedroom and closed the door. He had been waiting a long time to feel her body next to his again. Their lovemaking was incredible, and long overdue for both of them. He fell to the side of the bed and turned to say something romantic but roared with laughter. Madison had Bar-B-Q sauce all over her face. She looked at him and did the same. The sauce was smeared on his face as well.

She grabbed his face and started to lick it. "I think I'm going to get the ribs next time, they sure were good."

"I told you, you would like them," he chuckled. He got up and washed his face and dressed. He leaned down, kissed her forehead and then opened the door. He was so busy watching her; he nearly tripped over Sophie, who was waiting at on the other side of the door. Madison hollered, "Don't hurt my little Sophie."

Josh leaned down and picked up the little pup, "Sorry girl," he said as he carried her to the bed. She wagged her tail, then sat next to Madison as Josh left the room.

Madison washed her face and dressed, and then met him back in the kitchen. He wasted no time resuming his attack on the ribs, only this time he put a few into the box of Madison's Lo Mein.

She smiled and picked up her box of food. "Now where were we?"

"I was about to tell you that I didn't think the girlfriend was honest about telling Jon Smith she was okay with the roommate. Are you going to talk to her tomorrow?"

"Yes," she answered as she began eating.

"I know I'm not working with you on this case, but if there is anything I can help you with, I hope you won't hesitate to ask."

"Thank you, I will. Who knows, we might find a body somewhere and then we will be working together. Not that I want anyone to be dead. I didn't mean it like that."

"I caught what you meant," he smiled. "I'd better get out of here and let you get some rest. I'll see you tomorrow?"

"I'll call you after I talk with the girlfriend." She leaned into him and gave him a quick kiss.

Josh kissed her back and then turned and said goodbye to Sophie and left.

Madison watched as he drove off. Just as he made the turn he honked and waved. She waved back and then headed inside.

"I think you like him, don't you little girl?"

Sophie barked and started spinning around. "Okay, I know, you want to go outside." Sophie ran to the back door and sat and waited for Madison. She sauntered out to the small enclosed yard, sniffing for that perfect spot to do her business. Madison left the door slightly ajar so Sophie could get back in. She grabbed the box of leftover spare-ribs and plopped down on the couch. *Damn, that man can make love, but I'm sure not going to tell him how good he is or I'd never get that smile off his face.* She giggled as she finished off the ribs.

Sophie finally came back in and not a minute too soon. A flash of lightning struck and thunder roared. Sophie scooted for the bed before Madison could close the door. "It's okay, little girl."

She curled up under the covers with Sophie still shaking and pressing her little body against Madison. But it didn't take long before she settled down and was asleep. Madison looked down at her and gently slid her to one side so she could turn over. The sound of the rain beating on the roof was soothing, and Madison finally drifted off to sleep.

Chapter Four

Madison awoke to the aroma of the coffee dripping from her coffee pot. She slid out of the bed trying not to wake Sophie and made her way into the kitchen for that first cup of coffee. She forgot that she hadn't cleaned up from the night before. "Oh well, coffee first, then I'll clean up. It's not like I'm going to have company this hour."

The rain had gone but left a fog hovering over the backyard. She opened the French doors and walked outside to greet the morning. *There's something special about the early morning that just makes me feel life is all good. Maybe it's the silence before the hustle of the day.* She breathed in a deep breath of the fresh, misty air, stretched her shoulders and drew the steaming coffee to her lips. She let the steam rise into her face before taking another sip. *Life is good. I have my case, a hot cup of coffee, and I had great sex last night with a hunk of a guy. Now I call that good.*

She heard Becca next door opening her door. "Good morning, Becca. What are you doing up this early?" she asked as she walked over the wall between their yards.

"I just wanted to get an early start. I have a feeling about this case and I want to be prepared."

"What do you mean, you have a feeling?"

"I don't know; it's just one of those gut feelings I used to get when I worked for the attorney. It always turned out to be more than what we thought it was going to be. Not a run-of-the-mill case. I have the same feeling about this one. I don't believe it's going to be just a simple missing person."

Madison tilted her head and took another sip of coffee. "Not a simple one?"

"I didn't mean the case was simple. I meant I believe there are going to be some challenging events that will be in play with this one, and I like a challenge, don't you?"

"I do," Madison responded.

Becca turned and started back into her place. "See you later, Boss."

"Later," Madison called out.

By the time Madison had finished her first cup of coffee, Sophie was scurrying around the yard. Madison casually walked back into the kitchen, while glancing around at the mess she'd left, she poured another cup of coffee. "This is not me. I rarely go to bed without cleaning up the kitchen, but somehow, it just doesn't seem that important today." She curled up on the couch to finish her second coffee. She started mulling over what Becca said. *That sounded like something Jim Tucker would say. He would have a gut feeling about the cases he gave me, and he was right. I wonder if this one is going to be one of those weird, complex mysteries?*

Madison's cell phone rang; it was Josh. "Good morning. I guess you're already at the office."

"As a matter of fact, I'm sitting at home enjoying my second cup of coffee. What are you up to?"

"Excuse me, I thought I called P.I. Hart. I must have the wrong number," he snickered. "I can't believe you're not in the office staring at the board."

"As soon as I finish this cup and get ready, I plan to get there. Why, what's the big hurry?"

"Nothing, that just doesn't sound like the bulldog investigator I know."

"After spending time with Winter and just lounging around for two weeks, I guess I haven't got back into the swing yet. I'm sure once I hit on a clue, I'll be back to my old bulldog self."

"I didn't mean it as anything bad. I just know how you get on a case. You want me to come by the office with some of those great Krispy Kreme donuts that you love so much?"

"I'm pretty sure that you're the one that loves them so much, but hey, that does sound good this morning. I'll meet you there in about fifteen minutes. Don't eat them all before I get there. You know what I like."

"Oh yeah, I know what you like."

"I didn't mean *that*. I meant the kind of donuts I like."

"Got ya," he laughed.

She jumped in the shower, dressed and grabbed her bag and started for the door when she remembered she needed to set up Sophie's food and water, and set a few potty pads on the bathroom floor. When she finished, she patted Sophie on the head. "I'll be back in a little while. You be a good girl." Sophie immediately ran to the overstuffed chair and curled up, with her head on the armrest watching as Madison left.

The office was less than five minutes away. She kept telling herself she was going to start walking to work, but every time she began to, she thought, *what if I have to leave suddenly on a case. I'd have to run back to the house and get my car.* That was the excuse she would use to justify driving the one block away.

Josh and Becca were already at the office. They would usually be in the back room set up for the case, but since there wasn't much on this one yet, they were standing in the reception area. The minute she walked in, it was apparent Josh had already been in the donuts. He acted like he hadn't, but the white powdered sugar was still evident on his face. "I see you couldn't wait."

He scratched the top of his nose and looked down at the box of donuts, "I have no idea what you're talking about. I was waiting for you."

Madison shook her head and walked up to him and wiped the sugar off of his chin. "Yeah, I can see you did."

He grabbed at his face trying to catch any other evidence that might be lingering."But I didn't eat the kind you like."

She turned her head toward him as she reached for a donut and raised one eyebrow. All he could do was smile. It took everything in her not to laugh. He did look like a kid who got his hand caught in the cookie jar.

He quickly tried to change the subject. "So, when are you going to talk to the girlfriend?"

"I'm going over there this morning."

"Okay then." He waited for her to ask him to join her, but Madison said nothing about him coming along.

"I want to look at the board before I leave."

"Why does that not surprise me," he mumbled.

"What?" she asked.

"Oh, nothing."

"Becca, would you mind getting me the address, I want to get going on this?

"Yes, ma'am."

Madison headed to the back and Josh followed her. He stepped up to the board to read what she added. "Well, if the roommate's alibi pans out, you can cross him off as a person of interest."

"I don't cross anyone off until the case is closed," she mumbled. "But it does look like he doesn't know where his roommate went. I've been thinking about what you said in regards to the girlfriend. Why would she be okay if her boyfriend is living with such an attractive roommate? Well, I guess we'll find out."

"We?"

"If you don't have anything to do for the next couple of hours, I could use your help. You're better at interviewing women than I am. I always assume the worse, and that's what I get, but you have the charm with the ladies," she grinned.

Josh stood tall, adjusted his pants and ran his fingers through his hair. "You think so?" he beamed.

"Oh yeah. Remember how you charmed that wacko woman that tried to kill me, in our last case? She was definitely smitten with you," she chuckled.

"You sure know how to crush a guy, Ms. Hart."

"I'm just kidding you. You are better at interviewing people than I am. I would love to have your company. After all, it just wouldn't feel the same since we're so used to working together. But what about your *real* job as Detective of the Major Crime Division at the Maitland Police Departement? What would Chief Baker say?"

"I think he's glad I'm out of the office right now. Apparently I pace when we have no ongoing cases to solve, and we don't have anything major right now," he replied.

"I thought you told me your desk was full of cases."

Josh ignored her remark. "I've got a little spare time right now."

"Well then, let's go."

Madison headed out to Casselberry to talk to the girlfriend. They turned onto Red Bug Road and drove east about two miles to a small sub-division. They pulled up to a small Ranch style home, painted gray with charcoal shutters. Lavender Azaleas lined across the front of the house, against a perfectly manicured yard. Madison stepped up and rang the doorbell. A petite young woman with long black hair answered the door.

Josh showed her his badge, and they introduced themselves and then asked. "Are you Ginny Stapleton?"

"Yes, what's this about?" Ginny asked.

"We're working on a missing person's case and just had a few questions to ask you."

"I don't know how I can help. I only met her a couple of times when I was visiting my boyfriend. She stayed in her room most of the time when I was there."

"Can you tell us where you were last weekend?"

She crossed her arms and rested them against her chest. "Yes, I was here with Jon that weekend," she insisted.

"So, Jon is your boyfriend?" Josh asked.

"He is. We've been dating for almost a year."

"Jon never went out to the store for anything?" Madison asked.

Ginny rocked to one side. "No, we ordered pizza on Saturday, and Jon grilled steaks Sunday. We watched the game between the University of Florida and Florida State. Jon is a big Florida Gator fan."

"Did Jon stay with you all weekend?

She gave an exasperated sigh, "I just told you, he was with me *all* weekend. I'm feeling very uncomfortable with your questioning. I hope you don't think Jon had anything to do with her leaving. They weren't close, but she was helping out with the expenses, and I'm sure he didn't want her to leave and stick him with everything. Now, I think you'd better leave."

Madison leaned in and handed the woman her card. "If you can think of anything else, please give me a call. Her mother is very worried, and we would like to find this young lady."

Ginny looked at the card and relaxed her stance. "I'm sorry she's missing, but I'm sure Jon doesn't know where she is."

"Thank you for your time," Madison said as she turned to leave.

Ginny remained on the porch looking at the card as they got back in their car. Madison watched as Ginny walked back into the house. "I don't think she knows anything."

Josh shrugged his shoulders and turned toward Madison. "I thought you were going to question her about how she felt with her boyfriend living with another woman?"

Madison glared out the window as she drove off. "The timing didn't feel right. There will be another time."

"Okay," he mumbled.

Madison kept her eyes on the road. "I want to check Zoe's phone records, not just her cell phone, but her land-line too. Let's see if there has been any activity on either one lately. That's something you could check out for me."

"I was just thinking the same thing. I'll do that as soon as I get back. Would you drop me off at my car? I need to swing by the station and see if anything is going on. I'll call you later."

"Thank you, Josh. I appreciate that."

"No, problem," he smiled.

Madison let Josh off in front of her office, and she went inside. Becca followed Madison back to the case room. "How did it go with the girlfriend? Did you learn anything?"

"Not much. She was adamant about Mr. Smith being with her the entire time. I never asked her how she felt about Jon living with a beautiful young woman."

Becca put her hands on her hips, "Why not? I thought that was why you wanted to talk to her."

"I did. But after her defense of the guy, I thought I'd give her time to think about what we said. I want her to mull over the idea that we might suspect him of having something to do with the roommate leaving," Madison stated as she scratched the marker across the board.

"Oh, I see," Becca smiled. "Smart."

Madison jotted down the information Ginny Stapleton gave her on Jon's alibi under his name, and she stood back and stared at the board. "Not much to go on right now, but we're just beginning. Josh is checking out Zoe's phone records. That should tell us more about where she might be, and set up a timeline."

"I could have done that for you," Becca insisted.

"I know, and I was going to ask you, but I could tell Josh wanted to be a part of this investigation. I think he's bored right now."

"I think you're right. He misses the challenge and being your partner in crime, so to speak," Becca chuckled.

Josh returned to the Police Station. Not much had been happening in town lately to warrant his experience as a Crime Investigator, but the idea of working alongside Madison again brought back memories of how well they gelled on the last two cases. They were probably the most interesting and challenging crimes of his career, and he had a gut feeling her new case was going to more than some young woman moving out of her apartment to avoid her bills.

He swung open the door to the reception area. "Good morning, Detective Logan," Betty said.

He smiled. "Good morning, sweetheart."

"I guess I don't have to ask you what's keeping that smile on your face lately, do I?" she giggled.

"What are you talking about?"

"You know darn well what I'm talking about, Detective. A certain FBI Agent has returned to her hometown to pursue her own business, and I'll bet the farm that you're more than glad about it."

"Betty, we're just friends. Besides, I think we make a good team, just a working team. I have to admit, I wouldn't mind working another case with her, but right now she doesn't need any of my help."

"Hmm, that's how her cases start out, but we both know with Ms. Hart it could be much more. The woman is a magnet for discovering the dark side of secrets," Betty shuttered.

"You do have a point, but that's what makes working with her so much fun," Josh boasted.

"You are a bit morbid, Detective Logan."

"How long have we known each other, Betty?"

"I think it's been about eight years now, why?"

"What's my first name?"

"In this office, it's Detective," she said as she started shuffling through her papers.

Josh just shook his head and headed back to his office when he passed Chief Baker in the hall.

"How's Agent Hart's new case coming along?" Chief Baker asked.

Josh jerked his head back, raised one eyebrow and glared at the Chief, "I guess it's going okay, but why would you ask me?"

The chief grinned, shook his head and walked down the hall.

Am I that obvious about how I feel about Madison? What's happening to me? The woman is driving me crazy.

He opened the door to his office and started to ring Betty in the front to see if she could find out about the missing woman's phone records. *Oh, no you don't Josh, you don't need to flame the fire. Look them up yourself.*

After contacting the phone company, he found that the landline had been disconnected the weekend the girl went missing. Also, there had been no calls made from her cell phone since the Friday before she supposedly moved out. The last call Zoe McClain made from her cell was to a man. Josh wanted to call him, but it was not *his* case.

He called Madison. "Maddy, I got the information you wanted. I'm on my way over. I think you'll find this interesting."

"Okay."

Madison turned to Becca, "That was quick, and a bit curious. Josh is on his way back; he found out something."

"Did he say what it was?"

"No. He could have told me over the phone, but I think he likes to see new information get posted to our board," she grinned.

"I sure hope this case evolves into something the Maitland Police can officially get involved with, or that guy is going to get fired," Becca laughed.

Becca and Madison were in the back room, but could hear the squealing of Josh's brakes as he pulled into the parking spot. The front door flung open. "Hey, where is everyone?"

Madison poked her head out of the back room, "Where do you think we are?"

Josh rushed to the back as though he had the clues that would break the case. He gasped for breath, unbuttoned his jacket, opened his briefcase and spread his papers on the table. He gasped for breath. "Okay, her landline was shut-off Friday afternoon, but she made a call on her cell shortly before then to a David George. I did a little checking around and found out that he used to date our victim but the guy has no criminal record, and no alarms went off. But I think we should talk to him."

Madison stood there looking at him waiting for him to settle down. He finally sat down, took another deep breath and smiled up at her. "Well?"

Madison quickly turned her head. It was all she could do to keep from laughing. He was so proud of himself, and one would think it was his first case instead of being a fifteen-year police veteran.

Madison picked up the marker and started to scribble on the board. "Okay, let's add this guy, David George, to the board as a person of interest. Maybe he will be able to tell us more. I want to find out why he was the last person known to have talked to our missing girl and what he knows."

Madison placed the marker down on the table. "That sounds like a good place to start tomorrow. It's been a long day, and I'm hungry and tired."

Josh jerked his head back slightly, "What? Normally you would be knocking down the door to follow a lead."

Madison smiled, "Becca, lets's call it a day. Go home and get some rest and I'll see you back here in the morning. I'm sure Detective Logan would like to bring us some coffee and bagels, right Detective?"

"Uh, sure."

"Okay Boss, I'll see you tomorrow." Becca pulled her purse out of the bottom drawer of her desk and headed out the door. "See you tomorrow, Detective," she hollered.

"Yeah, tomorrow," he yelled back.

As soon as the door closed Josh stood up. "Is everything alright?"

Madison walked around the other side of the table and put her hands on his face. "Everything is fine, now let's get a bite to eat. Do you feel like grabbing something from the food trucks at Lake Lily?"

Josh shrugged his shoulders, tilted his head and grinned. "You're up to something, aren't you?"

"No, I just thought we'd take a break before we interviewed the ex-boyfriend," she snickered.

"But I thought…"

"That's what I wanted Becca to think too because she would have stayed until we returned from the interview, and I could see she was tired. She is so dedicated to this job, almost to a fault, and I don't want her to drive herself as hard as I do."

Josh threw his fists in the air and nodded his head. "So we are going to talk to the guy. I should have known that my Maddy wouldn't let a lead rest until morning."

She looked into his eyes, "Josh, I'm thrilled you want to be a part of this, but I don't want you jeopardizing your job over it."

"No chance of that, but thanks for caring. I'm going to tell you something for your ears only. The Chief told me to stay on this with you. He wants answers too. So I guess you could say we're working together again. But I know, it's your case."

"That makes me feel a lot better knowing Chief Baker is on board with this." She smiled, reached up and gave him a kiss.

"If I had known I'd get that, I would have told you sooner."

Madison slapped him on the arm, and he drew up. "Ouch!" he laughed. "You hit like a girl."

She raised one eyebrow and slightly tucked her chin, "I can do better if you'd like."

"That's okay, let's eat," he said making his way to the door.

There was a slight briskness in the air that night as they headed toward the vendors on Lake Lily. Madison stepped up to the Thai truck to order. "I can't believe how fast this year is going. It's almost October, and I'm on my third case with you."

Josh stood back until she got her food and walked over to the burger truck. "I'll have a loaded burger with everything but onions." He turned to Madison. "Yeah, we're on another case together. But I don't think this one will be as crazy as the last two. And besides this is just a missing lady who most likely just up and left," he said as he reached for his burger.

She winked at him as she took a bite of her Thai noodles. "I wouldn't count on that just yet. We never know where the clues will lead us."

They found an empty table near the bandstand by the lake. The same trio was playing that were playing the first time Josh and Madison ate there. "I guess we're becoming regulars here," he grinned as the mustard stuck to his lip.

Madison took her napkin and reached over and dabbed his mouth. "You sure wear your food well."

"I can't help it. It's your fault."

"Of course it is," she snickered.

They listened to the music for about a half hour longer. Josh tapped his foot to the rhythm when Madison nudged him, "I think we'd better go, we still have work to do."

"Oh yeah." He tossed their trash into the bin and started for the car. He seemed eager to hear what David George had to tell them. He jumped into the driver's side of the car before Madison could get to the door.

As she closed her door, she turned to him. "I wonder what the ex will have to say?"

"If they were no longer seeing each other, I'm curious about what they talked about and what their relationship was," Josh added.

David George lived in Oviedo, Florida, about twenty minutes from Zoe's apartment. On the way to his place, Madison called Zoe's mother to see what she had to say about Mr. George. "Mrs. McClain, this is Madison Hart. What can you tell me about David George and Zoe's relationship? I heard they once dated but remained friends."

"David and Zoe broke up quite some time ago but have remained good friends. Zoe considers David to be her best friend. Why are you asking about him?" Mrs. McClain said.

"We're just checking with everyone who knew your daughter. It's just part of our investigation. Mrs. McClain, did Zoe break it off with Mr. George or did he break it off with her?"

"Please, call me Denise. Well, she broke it off with him, but from what Zoe told me, they had been drifting apart for some time. She wanted to date other people, and I think he did too, but they continued to hang out together even after they broke up, but only as close friends. Zoe said she confided in David because he knew her so well."

Madison hesitated for a moment and then asked, "How was their relationship when they were dating? Did they argue much?"

"I never heard a sharp word between them, and Zoe never mentioned that they did. I was surprised when they broke up. He was such a perfect gentleman and was always nice to me. I thought maybe he was the one for Zoe. David calls me almost every day to see how I am and to find out if there has been any news on Zoe. He's as worried as I am."

"Thank you. I'll keep you posted if we find out anything," Madison said as she ended the call.

"Well, what did she have to say?" Josh asked.

"Seems as though they got along great, even after they broke up. I find that to be a little strange. You don't normally hang around with someone you just ended a relationship with. One party is usually harboring ill will. I am eager to get his take on their so-called friendship," Madison grumbled.

As they drove up to David's two-story home, they saw a man in the driveway cleaning out his car. Josh pulled into the driveway, and he and Madison approached Mr. George. Josh let Madison do the interviewing since it was still her case. "Good evening, are you David George?" she asked.

The man put the hose down, picked up a towel and dried his hands. "Yes, I am. What can I do for you," he said politely.

"I'm Madison Hart, and this is Detective Logan with the Maitland Police Department. We'd like to ask you a few questions about Zoe McClain. Do you have a few minutes?"

"Yes, of course. What do you want to know?"

Josh stood beside Madison with his chin up, chest out, one hand in his pocket and the other to his side, remaining quiet but studying Mr. George's every move.

"How well do you know Ms. McClain?" Madison asked.

"We're best friends," he stammered.

"When was the last time you talked to her?"

"I can't remember, but I got a message on my voicemail that she wanted to talk to me. She said something strange happened at work."

"When did you get that call?"

"It was the day before she went missing. I meant to call her back that day, but I got involved with a project at home and forgot to call. When I tried to call her back the next day, I got no answer. I didn't give it too much thought until she went missing. Is she alright?"

With a firm, authoritative voice, Josh asked. "So you haven't talked to her since then?"

"No. But you might ask around her workplace. Maybe someone there will know what was going on."

"Thank you for your time, Mr. George. If you can think of anything else, please give me a call," Madison said as she handed him her card.

They walked back to the squad car. Josh kept watching David's reactions. He stuck Madison's card into his pocket, picked up the hose and continued washing his car.

"He doesn't seem too concerned that his best friend is missing, does he?" Josh snarled.

Madison looked out the window at Mr. George as they drove out of the driveway. "No, he doesn't."

"I think tomorrow we might want to talk to some of Zoe's co-workers. If there was something odd going on someone might know what it was." Madison sighed. "I'm exhausted, but I'm not ready to call it a day. You want to come by for a glass of wine while I let Sophie out?"

Josh wiggled his eyebrows, "I thought you'd never ask, Ms. Hart," he smiled.

Chapter Five

Madison reached over her pillow expecting to pet Sophie that morning, but instead brushed her arm against the stubble on Josh's face. She turned over, and Josh was lying there smiling at her. "Good morning, beautiful. Did you sleep well?"

She rubbed her eyes and looked around the room. Sophie wasn't there on the bed the way she usually was. "Where's Sophie?"

"Uh…she's in the back yard. I let her out after I set up the coffee pot. I guess I know where I stand in this house," he joked.

"Josh, I'm not awake yet. I'm used to getting up and letting her out before I even hit the bathroom."

"Would you like a cup of coffee?" he asked.

"Yes, I'll drink it in the shower." Josh raises his eyebrow. Madison smiles, "Don't judge."

"I'm not judging," he chuckled.

She started toward the bathroom, then turned, and Josh was lying on the bed naked with his head propped up on his hand. *Damn, he looks good.* She closed the door behind her and turned on the shower. She cracked open the door slightly to see if he was still there, but he wasn't. She sighed a deep breath and stumbled into the shower.

When she finished dressing, she found Josh out on the patio sipping his coffee. She rushed to the French doors, grabbed his arm and looked over the backyard wall. "Get in here before Becca sees you."

"I'm decent," he chuckled. "Besides, I already said good morning to her."

Madison covered her face with her hands, "Oh, Great."

Josh ignored her gestures, "Are you ready for your second cup of coffee now?"

"Sure," she said shaking her head.

He handed her a steaming hot mug with Carmel Macchiato creamer. She clutched the mug with both hands, closed her eyes and slowly brought the coffee to her lips and sighed. "Ah, just the way I like it. You do make a good cup of joe."

"Thank you, ma'am, I think I do, too," he proclaimed.

He finished his cup, grabbed his jacket and started for the door.

"Where are you going?"

"I know how you like to ease into the morning, and I'm going home to clean up. I'll come by the office in about an hour with more coffee and bagels. Although, I don't know why you wouldn't rather have Krispy Kreme donuts?"

"As a matter-of-fact, I would rather have the donuts today," she replied cocking her head and grinning.

"You've got it, see you soon."

Sophie ran into the house as soon as she heard the door close. She gave out one bark, looked around and then jumped up next to Madison. "Okay, so Josh took your spot in the bed last night," she said as she petted Sophie.

She poured a mug to go, picked up her briefcase, patted Sophie and left for work. Becca's car was already parked in the driveway when she drove up. She opened the front door, "Good morning Becca," she said hoping Becca wouldn't ask about Josh.

"Good morning, Boss. I've updated the board, but I haven't added any new information. Let me know when you're ready for me."

Madison breathed a sigh of relief. She didn't want to explain why Josh was out on her patio that early in the morning. She scribbled a few things that David George then stood back and stared at the board. She was already three days into the investigation, but some interesting leads were surfacing. Suddenly, the front door of the office opened. "Hey, anyone here?" Josh hollered.

"We're back here. Becca, will you join us too, please."

Becca followed Josh to the back room. Becca squinted her eyes looking at the board. Josh twisted his head trying to make out what Madison had written.

Madison put her hands on her hips and looked at the both of them. "What is the problem?"

Josh scratched the top of his head. "Maybe you'd better leave the organization of the board to Becca. I can't make out what in the world you just wrote."

"Becca, you can read this, right?"

Becca bit her lower lip, clutched her chin in her hand, and leaned forward. "Well, sort of."

"Okay, Becca, would you mind cleaning up my chicken scratch writings?"

Becca took a sip of her coffee. "I'll take care of this after you two leave. I assume you have another lead to follow?"

Josh smiled. "Yes we do, thank you, Becca."

Madison got up, grabbed her coffee and started to the door. Josh started to laugh.

"What's so funny?" Madison asked.

Josh stepped up to her with a napkin and wiped the blotch of cream on her chin, and chocolate off the tip of her nose. Plus she had sugar down the front of her blouse from the donut she had eaten. "I can't take you out in public looking like that," he chuckled.

Madison bit her lip. "Seems we've had this conversation before, but it was the other way around. It was you wearing your food."

Madison turned to say something to Becca. Becca's face was bright red, and there were tears running down her cheeks as she tried to hold back her laughter. "Good luck on your leads today, Boss."

Josh looked back at Becca and winked, and she winked back.

Zoe McClain had landed a job as a first-grade teacher and from what her mother told Madison, she was looking forward to the new school year.

Madison and Josh walked into the principal's office. "Wow, does this bring back memories," Josh whispered.

"Good ones?"

"Not exactly."

Principle Shields entered the room. "Good morning Detective Logan," the principle said, extending his hand out.

"Good morning, Mr. Shields, this is Agent Madison Hart. She's working on a missing person's case that involves one of your employees."

"Yes, how can I help you, Agent Hart?"

"What can you tell us about Ms. McClain?"

"She stayed pretty much to herself last year, but this year she seemed to reach out more to some of her co-workers. I know she was excited about getting everything set up for the first day of school. Our second-grade teacher, Ms. Simpson, said Zoe was here all day setting up her classroom. The next day she didn't show up, and she didn't call either. We tried calling her several times but got no answer. You might want to talk to Angela. Her room is down this hall, the second door on the right," he said as he pointed in the direction of the classroom.

"Can you tell me which room was Ms. McClain's?" Josh asked.

"Yes, it's directly across the hall from Ms. Simpson's."

Madison stood up, "Thank you, Mr. Shields."

Principle Shields held the door as they exited his office. "If there is anything else I can help you with, feel free to call. We are all very concerned about Zoe."

Classes were just being let out for recess as Josh started to open the door. A mob of second-graders nearly trampled him. "Remember, walk don't run," the teacher yelled out to the children. Some of the kids barely slowed down, while most of them darted for the door. There was a teacher's assistant who ran up ahead to be with the children as they left the building.

Madison introduced herself and asked if Ms. Simpson had a moment.

"Not really, you caught me at a bad time. I can't take my eyes off these kids, or they'll be into something before I can blink. However, you can come outside with us if you'd like."

Madison and Josh followed the group to the playground. As soon as the children made their way through the doors, they went wild...running, climbing and chasing each other around the yard.

"How do you keep track of all of them?" Josh asked.

"Sometimes I don't. But that's why we have an assistance out here with us. Johnny, let go of Emily's hair. What did I tell you about how to treat girls?" she hollered across the yard.

"Sorry Ms. Simpson," Johnny yelled back.

"You certainly have your hands full with this group," Madison remarked.

"I apologize. How can I help you?" Ms. Simpson asked.

"We're looking into the disappearance of Zoe McClain. We'd like to know a little more about her and Principle Shields said you two were close," Madison replied.

"I wouldn't say we were close, but we did hang out together on our breaks. She's a dedicated teacher. But I'm afraid she didn't confide in me, or anyone else that I know. I'm sorry, but I don't think I can help you find her. Did you talk to her ex-boyfriend?"

"What about him?" Josh asked cautiously.

"Do you remember his name?" Madison added.

"Yes, it's David George. She did tell me that they talked on the phone often. I overheard her leaving him a message a few days before she left. She said she wanted to talk to him about something strange, but that's all I heard. She sounded upset, and when I asked her if everything was okay, she just nodded and changed the subject. I could tell that something was on her mind. After she had set up her classroom, I walked with her to her car. She barely said a word all the way out to the parking lot, and that was the last time I saw her. Is she alright?"

"That's what we're trying to find out. If you think of anything else, please give me a call." Madison handed her a card.

"I will. I sure hope she's okay," Ms. Simpson mumbled as she looked down at the card.

Madison and Josh got back into the car and headed back toward Maitland. "Hey Maddy, I'm beginning to think this girl didn't just up and leave. Somebody knows what happened to her; we just have to find out who."

"I was thinking the same thing. So far, the only thing indicating she might have moved is that all her belongings are gone. There is no activity on any of her accounts, no calls out from her cell phone and no one seems to have any idea where she went. A woman who spends an entire day setting up her classroom to teach just doesn't up and leave. I hate to admit it, but I think she may have met with foul play."

"Yeah, it looks that way, but we're not going to give up trying to find her, dead or alive," Josh vowed.

"I need to talk to Zoe's mom again, but I want to check on a few more things before I do. Let's head back to the office."

Madison opened the door to the office, and Becca was on the phone. She raised her finger to motion them to stay there. All Madison could hear was, "Okay, we'll check into that right away." And then Becca hung up. "I've been receiving calls all morning. Apparently, Mrs. McClain has spent the last few days with family and friends putting up missing person's posters about Zoe. I just received another call saying they think the woman on the poster is sitting in her coffee shop right now. I was just getting ready to call you when you walked in. Here is the name and address of the coffee shop. The woman who called said she's going to try and keep her there until you arrive. I asked her if she would take an inconspicuous photo with her cell." Becca showed the photo to Madison and Josh reached for the paper, and then they darted out the door. Madison turned to Becca, "Great work."

Josh sped down Highway 17-92 toward the Sanford/Orlando Airport. There was a small coffee shop and gas station just off the highway. Madison could see a petite young woman with long flaming red hair sitting there having coffee. Her heart started racing, and she picked up her pace. From a distant it sure looked like the photo of Zoe that her mother gave Madison. Josh entered the coffee shop, and the bell rang over the door. Madison walked to the counter, and Josh showed his badge. "You just called in regards to our missing person?" Madison whispered.

The waitress leaned across the counter, "She's sitting alone over there in the booth."

They slowly walked to the booth. Madison drew close but didn't want to spook the young lady. If this wasn't Zoe, it could be her twin. Madison took a long deep breath and then spoke, "Excuse me, are you, Zoe McClain?"

The young woman turned and looked at both of them. "Who are you?"

"I'm Agent Hart, and this is Detective Logan from the Maitland Police Department. Are you Zoe McClain?"

"No. My name is Cynthia Overstreet. I'm just waiting for my husband and children to join me."

"Do you have any identification with you?" Josh asked calmly.

The young woman reached into her purse and pulled out her wallet. She handed him her driver's license, and it read, Cynthia Overstreet. About that time, a man and two small children came into the coffee shop. The children ran up to the woman, "Mommy, look what Daddy got us," one child said showing her a stuffed hippo. The husband approached the table with his eyes narrowed, furrowing his eyebrows. "Cynthia, what's going on?"

Madison introduced herself. "We had a call about a missing person, and your wife is the spitting image of the woman we're looking for, so we had to follow up. Thank you for helping us clear this up."

The husband sat down next to his wife and the children jumped into the booth. The woman looked up at Madison. "I sure hope you find the woman you're looking for."

"Thank you, we do too."

They left the café and got back into the car.

"Well, that was a bust," Josh grumbled.

"For a brief moment, I thought we found her."

There were several other sightings and leads from the posters. But none of them panned out, however, they still had to follow up on each one. By the end of the day, they were both dragging and exhausted.

Days went by with nothing solid.

Madison and Josh had gone over every lead. Becca had re-written the board several times, but this case was going nowhere. Madison stood staring at the board."I can only imagine the anguish Zoe's mother must be going through right now wondering where her daughter is. With no clues and no one hearing from Zoe after this amount of time, I'm afraid the outcome is going to be grim."

"Okay, let's start from the beginning. Becca, would you mind bringing in the box of Zoe's belonging?"

Becca carried in the box of papers found in her trash and a few items that remained in Zoe's apartment. She spread them on the table and began to go through every scrap of paper. Madison found a crumpled up invitation to an event. It was a hand-written invitation and looked personal. It didn't look like Zoe was interested in the event, but Madison wanted to know who sent it and why. On the back of the card was the name and address of the person who sent it.

Madison leaned back in her chair. "I don't think I could talk to another person this evening, but why don't we interview this guy in the morning. Are you up for that?"

Josh slumped into the chair at the table and dropped his head into his hands. "I know what you mean. I don't think my brain could come up with any more questions to ask anyone right now. I think I'm just going to call it a day, jump in the shower and have a beer. I'll see you ladies in the morning. Oh, I forgot I have a briefing with Chief Baker at 8:00 a.m. concerning your case. I'll bring coffee and bagels over when we finish. The meeting shouldn't take long since we have nothing new." Josh stood up with his head lowered and slowly walked to the front to leave.

Madison was tempted to follow him out but didn't. She could tell Josh was worn out, and so was she.

"You both have been going at this non-stop for days. Why don't you call it a day too and go home? We can get a fresh start in the morning," Becca insisted.

Madison put down the papers, picked up her handbag and started for the door. "Yeah, you're probably right. I just hate not having anything concrete to tell Mrs. McClain about her daughter."

"Well, maybe this new clue will lead to something. You'll feel better in the morning," Becca smiled.

"Thanks, Becca."

Madison drove to her place, and when she opened the door Sophie spun around as though she hadn't seen her in days. "Sorry, baby. Your mommy is too tired to play," she said as she tossed her bag on the counter and then opened the French door for Sophie to go outside. She walked back to the kitchen, opened the empty fridge and just stood there and stared. "I'm too tired to eat." She fixed Sophie a bowl of chicken, and set a fresh bowl of water on the floor, and then poured a glass of wine and plopped on the couch.

She kept thinking about the hand-written invitation found in Zoe's trash. "Why would she toss it? It looked like it was from someone special. Enough of this tonight, Madison. Let it rest. It's still going to be there in the morning," she muttered.

She sipped her wine, and before she knew it, she had fallen asleep on the couch with the French doors wide open.

The wind started to howl, and rain was blowing sideways in through the open doors. Madison thought she was dreaming until the crack of lightning and thunder hit nearby and woke her. She bolted from the couch to close the doors. She called for Sophie, but she didn't come. The backyard gate was closed, and she knew Sophie would not have stayed outside, but to be sure, Madison went out back to look for her. By the time she got back to the French doors she was sopping wet, and there was Sophie curled up on the overstuffed chair watching Madison. "Girl, you made me worry," Madison cooed as she bent down to pick the pup up. She placed

Sophie on the bed, disrobed and dried off before climbing into bed.

The next morning she awoke early still thinking about the case and the worry that Denise McClain must be enduring. She wanted to get to the office right away and to check out this guy who sent the invitation. She arrived before Becca, which was unusual. She walked to the back room. Becca had reorganized the board again. "How does she do it?" Every person's name who they had talked to was written on the board. Under each name, the details that pertained to Zoe were added. A timeline was slowly developing.

Madison hadn't been in the office more than ten minutes when Becca arrived. "Good morning, Boss. I hope you got a good night's sleep," she said as she put her purse in the bottom drawer of her desk.

"I fell asleep on the couch and left the doors open until that storm woke me. But after that I slept through the night. How about you? I see you stayed a little longer last night and re-did the board."

"Just trying to make your job easier, Boss," she smiled.

"Well, it does. Thank you."

"Are you and Detective Logan interviewing the man who wrote the invitation today?"

"That's the plan. Josh should be here around 9:00 a.m. with coffee and bagels, and then we'll head out to talk to this guy. From the way the invitation was written, it sounds like they may have had something going on between them. He might give us more of insight into Zoe. At least I hope so. I need to give Mrs. McClain something and soon."

"I Googled the guy last night and found out a few things about him," Becca said as she approached the board.

"You Googled him? Josh is right, I need to give you a raise…soon." She laughed.

"Well, there wasn't much to find out. He belongs to a couple of Geek groups, but he doesn't sound like the kind of fella that Zoe would find interesting. He's been living at the same address for over thirty years. I suspect he either still lives with his parents or lives in the same house where he grew up. I'll be eager to see what sort of character he is," Becca added.

"Maybe that's why Zoe tossed the invitation. We'll know more when we talk to him today."

"Hey, is anyone here," Josh hollered.

"We're back here," Madison called back.

"Can I get a hand, here?" he said as he tried juggling the coffees and bagels.

Becca darted to the front and took the box of coffees, and not a minute too soon. The box was breaking up, and he was about to drop them.

"How did your briefing go with Chief Baker?" Madison asked.

"He wanted to know if we had any solid leads. I told him we were following up on one this morning. He'd like to talk to both of us when we get back."

"I hope he's not going to pull you off of our case," Madison responded.

"No, I don't think that's what it's about, or I would have picked up on that at the briefing."

Madison sighed, and took a cup of coffee.

"I see Becca straightened and updated the board again," he chuckled.

"She did."

"So who is this Stephen Clark you have written on the board?" he asked.

Madison nodded at Becca.

Becca stepped up to the board. "This is the man that sent the invitation. I Googled him last night and jotted down what I discovered on the board so you two would have a little background on him this morning."

"Well done, Ms. Assistant. Has Madison given you that raise yet?"

Madison raised one eyebrow and gave him the look. "Not yet, but she might replace you."

He widened his eyes, twisted his mouth and cautiously reached for his coffee. "Oops, I'd better keep my mouth shut, or I'll be losing my partner."

"We've got work to do, let's get going," Madison stated as she headed for the front.

"Becca, call me if anything new comes up."

"Will do, Boss."

They pulled into the drive-through at McDonald's and ordered two more black coffees. Madison suggested that they stop by the school to talk to some of Zoe's co-workers first. She wanted to know if Zoe had ever mentioned Stephen Clark to any of them.

Principle Sheilds approached them in the hall. "Hello again, Detective Logan, Agent Hart. Have you found Zoe yet?"

Josh didn't answer him. He got right to the point. "Did Zoe ever mention a Mr. Stephen Clark to you?"

"Stephen Clark? No, that name does not sound familiar to me, but you might check with her co-workers again."

"Thank you," Madison said as they started back to the classrooms. Zoe's friend, Ms. Simpson, was just leaving her classroom.

Madison called out to her. "Ms. Simpson."

She turned, and when she saw it was Madison, she clutched her chest. "Did you find her?"

Madison shook her head, "I'm sorry, we haven't. But we will. Did Zoe ever mention a Stephen Clark?"

"She sure did. The guy is a wacko, and she couldn't get rid of him. He called her all the time. She blocked his number but somehow he found out a way around it and called her again. He sent her gifts, but she returned them. I know he sent several love letters to her. She finally started tossing them in the trash the moment they arrived. She never gave him her address, but he knew it. Maybe that's why she left. I remember she did write him one time and asked him not to write or call anymore. I'm not sure if that ended it or not."

Madison looked at Josh and then back at Ms. Simpson. "Thank you, if you can think of anything else, please call me.

"I sure will."

Madison and Josh got back in the car and headed for Clark's home. "Sounds like this guy is a stalker," Josh suggested.

Madison turned to him, "Why didn't she report him? Surely she knew there are stalking laws and that might have ended him bothering her."

Stephen Clark lived in a small community next to a trailer park. The paint on the house was chipping off, the enclosed wooden fence around the front yard was busted in several places, and the gate was hanging on one hinge. The grass nearly came up to the height of the fence. Every curtain across the front of the house was closed. The front porch barely had enough room to pass through to the door because of the clutter. Josh shrugged his shoulder and crinkled his nose. "Are you sure this is the address? I wonder if anyone lives here."

"This is the address we found." Madison knocked on the door several times. They were just about to turn around and leave when they heard the door crack open.

There stood a man about five feet, four inches tall, and dressed in a plaid shirt that was buttoned wrong. He was wearing navy blue pants at least three sizes too big with a belt that gathered the pants to hold them on. He reached up and pushed his black horn-rimmed glasses up from his nose. "Yes, may I help you?"

Josh approached him and showed him his badge and introduced himself and Madison.

Madison added that they were investigating the disappearance of Zoe McClain. "We found an invitation in her place to an event. Was that from you?"

"Of course, Zoe and I are very close," he slurred.

Josh glanced at Madison and narrowed his eyes. "Where did you two meet?"

"Would you like to come in?" He motioned for them to enter and then stumbled to one side, kicking a box to make room for them to pass.

Josh stepped in first, and Madison followed. The inside was even worse than the outside, and it smelled of old rotted garbage. There were unopened boxes stacked covering the floor, and bookcases crammed with cartoon memorabilia on every shelf. "Are you a collector?" Josh inquired.

"Oh yes, I have every comic book and action figure dating back thirty years. Mom thought I was wasting my money, but someday this will be worth a fortune. I just need to get it cataloged," he boasted.

"Does your mother live here with you?" Josh asked.

Mr. Clark lowered his head and softly said, "She passed away."

"I'm sorry for your loss."

"Thank you." Then he continued to show Josh his collections.

While he was showing Josh around, Madison shook her head. *How in the world did Zoe get involved with this guy?* "Mr. Clark, how did you meet Zoe?"

"We met online. I responded to her post, and the rest is history. We hit it off right away. We talked almost every day."

"Have you ever met her in person?" Madison cautiously asked.

"She's very busy, but I plan to take her to the Comic-Con next month. I sent her the invitation; she just hasn't had time to send it back to me yet. She and I, well...dare I say, are in love."

"In love?" Josh blurted.

"Yes. I know what you're thinking. I'm a little older than she is, but age makes no difference with us."

Madison nudges Josh on the arm. "Thank you for your time, Mr. Clark. If you can think of anything else, please give Detective Logan a call," Madison said as she nudged Josh again.

"Yes, here's my card," Josh said as he handed him the card.

"Detective Logan, when you see Zoe, tell her I can't wait until our date to the Comic Con."

Josh just nodded and slightly smiled. "Sure."

Madison could hardly wait to get out of that house. She sat in the car with her hand over her nose. "Good grief, I think I'm going to have to shower and wash my hair now. That guy is totally delusional, but could his imaginary world been crushed, and he do harm to Zoe? I don't know about that. I want to talk to some of her friends and see what else she said about this guy. Also, I want to see if he has a mental illness that may attribute to his state of mind.

"Yeah, he might have been on something, or heavily medicated. I could use another cup of coffee, how about you?" Josh asked. "When I get back to the station, I'll see what Betty can dig up on the guy. I know Becca could do some research, but Betty has access to police records.

"Yes, that coffee sounds good right now. Maybe it'll burn off the stench in my throat. I'm still going to have Becca do some research as well. She had connections when she worked for the attorney that might help. As much as we can find out about Mr. Clark, the better."

Josh pulled up to the window of the drive-through to order coffees, "I agree. Black?"

"Uh? Oh, the coffee, yes, black, and you'd better get one for Becca too, or you'll never hear the end of it," she chuckled.

"That's the truth. She'd make a great interrogator. She'd scare the pants off of the suspect."

"She has been a God-send for me, but I'm afraid I might lose her someday."

"Why would you say that?"

"Because I think she'd be good in the field and I'd rather her be working for me in that capacity than have her leave."

"She sure is detailed oriented, but I wouldn't worry about that anytime soon. I happen to know she's very dedicated to you. Maybe she could do both?"

"Yeah, maybe so," Madison smiled.

They pulled into the driveway of the office, and before they could get out of their car, Becca was standing at the door. "Hey you two, you don't have time to come in. I just got a call that a man found several items in a dumpster a few days after Zoe went missing that could belong to her." She grabbed the coffee from Josh and handed him a piece of paper with the address. "Thanks for the coffee."

Madison started to get back into the car, she held onto the door and called out to Becca, "Becca, would you mind seeing what you can dig up on Stephen Clark while were gone?"

"I'm on it, Boss."

Josh jumped back into the car and tried to place his coffee cup into the holder and missed, spilling coffee onto his lap. "Oh, this is going to look good when the Detective steps up to ask questions." He bellowed.

"Ah, they'll just think you're excited about the case," Madison laughed.

"Very funny, Maddy. Do we have time for me to swing by the house and change?"

"NO! Suck it up Detective and let's go."

Josh jerked his head back and backed out of the driveway. Madison pulled the paper napkins from the back seat and started dabbing the coffee spilled on his lap.

"I don't think that is a good idea."

"It will dry faster."

"Yeah, but then I'll have another problem if you keep that up."

"Keep your mind on the case, Logan," she grinned.

"Easy for you to say," he mumbled

They pulled up to an apartment close to Zoe's. Josh knocked on the door and an elderly lady answered it. "Are you the people I called about what I saw?"

"Yes, ma'am. I'm Agent Hart, and this is Detective Logan. Can you tell us what you saw?"

"Well certainly, but I can't stand for too long as my arthritis is kicking up today. Won't you come in and have a seat?" She motioned for them toward the living room. She had a plate of cookies set out on the coffee table and a teapot with three cups placed on a tray. "I don't get many visitors at my age. Most of my friends are deceased. Would you like some tea?" She started pouring the tea before they had a chance to decline.

Madison smiled, "Thank you." And then she nudged Josh.

Josh reached over the table as she handed him a cup of tea.

"I just made these cookies, take one of these with your tea."

Madison was eager to hear what she had to say.

"Can you tell me what you saw?"

She set her cup down and lowered her head, "Oh, I'm sorry, I almost forgot why you were here. Well, I was taking my trash out last week and noticed one of the maintenance workers, Charlie, sorting through some boxes of trash. I think some of those items belonged to the young lady who lived in that apartment down the way. I spoke to her a time or two, a lovely lady. I think she said she teaches school, or… now where was I? Yes, the boxes looked like the same ones I'd seen her carry into her place."

"You remembered a box?" Josh questioned.

"Yes, because she bought a new TV and some other things for her apartment. They were the same boxes the worker was rummaging through. He took several items, and if I'm not mistaken, one of them was the young lady's TV. Now, why would she toss away her new TV?"

Madison took a sip of tea and set her cup down. "Can you remember anything else he might have taken?"

"Not really, but he loaded several boxes into his truck that day."

Madison stood up, reached over and took the lady's hand. "Thank you for the tea and cookie. If you think of anything else, you can call us."

The old lady smiled at Madison. "You can come again anytime. You two make such a lovely couple."

Madison bit her lower lip and forced a smile. Josh blurted out, "Thank you, I think so too." He turned and winked at Madison. She grabbed his arm, "It's time to go sweetie."

The dark, heavy clouds quickly had rolled in and suddenly it began to pour. They still wanted to talk to the maintenance man before they left. They drove around the complex until they located his shop at the back of one of the buildings.

Josh turned around and grabbed his Gator umbrella, jumped out of the car and ran around to the front of the car to cover Madison as she got out. They darted into the shop. There was a scruffy looking man in his late forties standing at a table working on some locks. When he saw the two running in it startled him, and he grabbed a wrench and held it up in defense. Josh lowered his umbrella and aimed it at the man. Madison whispered, "Oh great, you're going to get him with that 8mm umbrella, right?"

"Charlie Foster?"

He lowered the wrench. "Yeah, who wants to know?"

"I'm Agent Hart, and this is Detective Logan. We understand you found some items in the dumpster the other day."

"I didn't steal them. Someone tossed them in there. I didn't do nothin' wrong."

"Would you mind setting that wrench back on the table." Josh impressed, pointing to the wrench.

"Sorry, Dude but we've had a few thefts and break-ins lately, and you startled me."

Josh spotted a few items in the back of the shop that looked similar to what Zoe's mother said were in the apartment. "Mind if we look around?"

"You got a warrant?"

"Is there something in here you don't want us to see?"

"No, but cops are always lookin', and if they can't find it, they plant it. At least that's what I heard."

Josh put his hands on his hips, pulling back his jacket just enough to expose his weapon. "That's fine. We can get a warrant, but when we do a team will tear this place apart. How happy is that going to make your boss?"

"Yeah, fine, dude. Go ahead and look around, but you ain't goin' find anything illegal in here."

Madison walked toward the back of the shop and looked into a large box, stuffed with woman's personal items. "Whose are these?"

He glanced to the side, rubbed his eyes and tightened his lips. "I found that stuff in the dumpster."

Madison continued to pull out items when she noticed a small ornate bedside table setting near the back corner of the shop. She picked up the table and carried it over to Charlie. "This is a pretty fancy table to have in a shop."

"So?"

She looked up at Josh and back to Charlie. "I'm afraid we're going to have to take these for awhile. Did you find anything else in the dumpster that isn't here in the shop?"

He wiped his brow with a handkerchief, lowered his head and put his hands in his coverall pockets. "I don't know."

Josh stepped up closer to Charlie. "What do you mean, you don't know? You either found something else or you didn't. Which is it?"

He shuffled his feet and blew out his cheeks. "I mean, I don't know what else I got. I might have sold a few things at the flea market. You ain't goin' tell my boss, are ya?"

Josh just shook his head and turned around and picked up the box Madison found. "Don't be going anywhere anytime soon...Dude."

"No sir, I won't. Where would I go, I live here in the back."

Madison swung around, "You live here in the shop?"

"Yes, ma'am."

"Do you mind showing me your place?"

"Uh, it's kinda a mess right, now. Can you come back later?"

Madison cocked her head. "If we have to come back later, you know what that will mean."

"Okay, but if there is anything illegal in there, it ain't mine. I had some guys over the other night, and they may have left something."

Josh interjected, "We're not looking for anything illegal."

Charlie took a deep breath and guided them to the back room. It was an old storage room he had converted to a bedroom and a small kitchenette area. It also had a tiny bathroom with a shower. He had a fairly new couch and a couple of modern lamps that did not look like they fit his profile. Sitting on top of a black, ornate dresser was a brand new 42-inch flat screen TV. None of these items appeared to be things he could afford or would pick out for himself, except maybe the TV. There was left-over pizza on the floor next to the couch, empty beer bottles on the coffee table, and ash residue in a pie tin used as an ashtray. The place smelled like marijuana. It was obvious the guy had been smoking in there.

Madison walked over to the couch and snapped a picture with her cell phone. She also took a photo of the lamps, TV, and a few other items in the room that didn't look like they belonged. "Where did you get your furniture?"

Charlie started rubbing his hands together, and sweat was running down his face. "A friend gave them to me."

Madison knew he was lying, but she wanted to verify her hunch before saying anything else. "Very nice."

She and Josh turned and walked out of the shop. Charlie leaned up against his workbench. His knees were shaking uncontrollably. He couldn't move. He just watched as Madison and Josh carried a few items out to their car.

Josh returned and handed him his card. "If you can think of anything else you might have seen or found, give me a call. We might need to talk to you again, so don't go anywhere and don't get rid of anything either."

Charlie attempted to take the card, but his hands were sweating and trembling. Josh reached around him and placed the card on the table and left.

They got into the car and started back to the office with some of the items. On the way, Madison sent the photos to Zoe's mother to see if she recognized anything.

Josh turned to her, "I'm not sure what he's hiding, but he's not telling us everything. We need to do some checking on his guy."

Madison's suspicions were gnawing at her. "If Zoe moved, why wouldn't she have taken her furniture and personal items? Josh, this isn't looking good."

"I know, I was thinking that too. She wouldn't leave all her new furniture behind if she were moving."

Suddenly Josh's stomach let out a loud growl. Madison jerked her head toward him and chuckled, "Are you hungry?"

"Was that me? I thought that was you making that noise."

"Seriously, Josh?"

"Well, we didn't get a chance to eat those bagels this morning. I might be a little hungry. You know where we haven't gone in a long time?"

"No, where?"

"You and I haven't been back to the Breakfast Club off of Maitland Avenue. Do you feel like grabbing a bite before we head back?"

"If I don't want to listen to your belly roar all day, we'd better."

They turned down Highway 436 off 17-92 and then onto Maitland Avenue. The Breakfast Club was a small diner nestled in the corner of a strip-mall. It was a casual place with friendly staff and reasonably priced food. The restaurant had it's regulars who ate there most mornings or gathered there for coffee.

Josh opened the door for Madison and they stepped in. "Hello, you two," someone hollered from behind the counter. Lisa had been working there as a waitress since they opened and knew everyone that frequented the diner. Madison and Josh met her during their last case. She knew more about her customers than Google could find, and she remembered every detail. "Where have you two been? Ms. Hart, I thought you returned to DC after that last case. That was some case, wasn't it? Oh, that's right, I heard you've opened up a private investigation agency on Swoope Avenue, in Maitland. It looks like your favorite table is empty. I'll get you both some coffee."

Madison swung her head back and glared at Josh. "That woman would put an elephant's memory to shame. If I need to know anything about anybody, all I need to do is ask Lisa."

Josh shook his head. "That's for sure; she never forgets a thing. It's been a while since we ate here. Was it on our last case?"

"Yes, over a month ago," Madison replied.

Lisa returned to the table with two coffees. She smiled and pulled out her order pad. "Are you two having your usual, or is Agent Hart going for the big pancake breakfast again?"

Josh's eyes widened, and a smirk crossed his lips, "Well, Agent Hart?"

She turned toward Josh, and lifted one eyebrow. "You know what, Lisa. I think I will go for the big one today."

"Okay then. How about you Detective, the usual?"

He sat straight up in the booth and lowered his chin, looking over at Madison. "I'll have my usual."

"Comin' up."

Josh couldn't take his eyes off of Madison. Her words conjured up a vision he shouldn't share in public, and his body was about to rise to the occasion. He dropped his napkin on his lap, grinned and whispered, "Woman, you sure have a way with words."

She reached over and took his hand and smiled. "Later I'll have more than words for you, now drink your coffee and get your mind on something else or we're going to have to sit here for quite a long time."

He pulled her hand to his lips and kissed her fingertips. "I can't wait."

For the first time, she did not come back with a sarcastic remark, nor did she pull her hand away. He looked into her eyes and saw a twinkle of warmth and tenderness. *Is she softening? Is my Maddy falling for me?*

Lisa approached the table and then Madison quickly jerked her hand back and pretended nothing happen. "Thank you, Lisa."

"Your food will be out in a minute. Would you like more coffee?

Josh looked up at Lisa, "We would. Thank you."

When Lisa left, Madison leaned across the table. "Josh, we need to concentrate on the case. If I want people to take me seriously as an investigator, we don't need to be acting like two love-struck school kids."

She said love-struck. He leaned back in the booth and snickered. "Yes, ma'am, I promise, no more public displays of affection, okay?"

"Thank you. Now, let's get back to the case. Doesn't that maintenance man usually have master keys to all the apartments?"

"Yes, he does. Where are you going with this?"

"Well, suppose he knew that the roommate was going to be out all weekend, and he let himself in, made a move on Zoe and things quickly went south and he killed her?"

Josh took a big sip of coffee. "Yeah, and he had to make it look like she moved, so he cleaned out the place, tossing most of her belonging into the dumpster. But went back for a few things that he thought might have incriminated him."

Madison sat quietly for a moment contemplating what Josh said.

"Maddy, what are you thinking?"

"Something doesn't feel right about that scenario, but I don't want to rule him out. I want to run by the office and start putting together our timeline and profile. One thing is becoming clear, and I don't like what it feels like."

Josh nodded his head, "Zoe didn't move willingly."

"I don't think so."

Chapter Six

They returned to the office, and Becca was on the phone as they walked in. Her eyes were red and welled up with tears. She hung her head, and her voice responded to the person at the other end in almost a whisper.

Madison's heart sank. It could not be good news. Josh stepped up close to Madison, and they waited for Becca to get off of the phone.

"Becca, what is it?" Madison said the moment Becca hung up.

Becca stood up, took a deep breath. "That was Chief Baker. He said he had been trying to reach the both of you and wants you out at the airport as soon as possible. The chief said they may have found Zoe's car."

Josh pulled out his phone, and it was on mute. "Damn," He walked into the back room and called the chief. "Chief, this is Logan. I must have pushed the mute button. What can you tell me?"

Madison could hear only silence from Josh. Something was going on. She was ready to get to the airport. Becca turned to Madison. "Boss, I have a real bad feeling about this. My gut tells me we're going to be working on more than a missing person's case. What are we going to tell her mother?"

Madison put her hand on Becca's shoulder. "Let's not jump to conclusions. She still may be alive." But she didn't believe what she was telling Becca. Madison handed Becca the notes she had on Charlie Foster. "While we're gone, I'd like you to start a timeline and add this information to the board. Also, find out all you can on this Charlie Foster. I want to know where he's from, any records on him, and who he hangs out with. Everything you can on him."

"Do you think he had something to do with Zoe's disappearance?"

"I don't know but if he didn't have anything to do with it, he knows something he's not telling us, and I want to know what it is."

Josh came running from the back. "Let's go."

They jumped into the squad car and raced down Highway 17-92 back toward Sanford/Orlando International Airport. It was about a fifteen-minute ride.

"Is the Chief upset with you?"

He kept his eyes on the road and his foot heavy on the gas. "No, but he sent another team out there to rope off the area until we get there. He wants us on this."

"How did they know it was there?"

"When Zoe's mother filed a missing person's report, the FBI put out a BOLO on the license plate."

Madison nodded her head. "Of course, then the license was automatically entered in the licence-trackers. An officer must have driven around in the parking lot, and their meter went off."

"Exactly."

"The Chief said there was no one in the car. They're waiting for us to check out the scene."

Josh pulled into the long-term parking and saw they had roped off the area immediately. The officers from

Seminole County had secured the site. He showed an officer his badge and Madison showed her FBI identification and badge as well. Madison looked at the car and turned to Josh. "Does that car look strange to you?"

"It sure does."

Josh hollered out to the officers, "Has anyone touched this car?"

"No sir," they responded.

He and Madison walked around to the back of the car. Josh stepped back to get a full view of the car. "Does it look heavier in the back?"

It didn't take long, and Madison answered, "The back end of this car is weighted down." A lump settled in her gut. Josh slowly walked up to the trunk. "Hey, do one of you guys have a crow-bar?"

"Yes, sir," one of the officers said. He pulled one out of his car and handed it to Josh.

Madison grabbed Josh's arm. "Josh," she said pointing to the ground beneath the trunk.

"What is that?"

There was a strange liquid dripping from the trunk. Josh leaned down to have a closer look. It was foul smelling. Josh took off his jacket, rolled up his sleeves and placed the crowbar under the trunk lid. He wedged into the lock and snapped it. The trunk popped open.

Madison stepped up next to him, as he slowly lifted the trunk. "What the hell?" Josh snapped.

Madison looked at the parking attendant. "How long has this car been here?"

"I guess for about two weeks," he replied.

"And you never notice anything strange?"

"No, ma'am, but there are a lot of cars in this lot, and I don't stop at every one of them."

Madison just shook her head.

Josh pulled out his cell phone and shot several pictures and then he turned to Madison. "What is this?"

"She got closer. "It's dirt, and it looks like cat litter. This person knew the kitty litter would mask the odor of the decomposing body.

Josh brushed away some of the dirt. "Is that a shoe?"

Madison put on her latex gloves and brushed more of the dirt aside. "Josh, you might want to call Doc Webb. I think there's a body under this."

"As soon as Doc Webb examines the body, we'll send the entire car to the crime lab." Josh closed the trunk. "I don't want to disturb any evidence. It will limit those prints we find and who we can eliminate right off. I need to call the Chief."

Madison waited by the car while Josh called the chief to make arrangements for them to haul the car to the lab.

When Josh got hung up the phone, he turned to Madison. "Are you going to call Mrs. McClain?"

"There's no need to call her until we know who this is in her daughter's car. We can't be sure its Zoe until Doc tells us it is. I don't want to worry her any more than she is already, especially if it isn't her daughter. This is the part of this business I hate. It never gets easy telling a family member that a loved one is dead. No, I won't say anything to Denise until we have all the facts."

Josh lowered his head. "Yeah, she's upset enough just knowing her daughter is missing. I guess you're going to want to meet Doc at the lab as soon as possible, but you know he won't have anything for a while. It's going to take some time just remove whatever this is from the trunk, then the autopsy. Let's swing by the station and then take a break."

"If this is Zoe, we won't be taking any breaks."

"Maddy, there's nothing we can do until Doc finds out who this is. There will be plenty for us to do as soon as we know, so in the meantime, let's go over what we have, and then take a break."

"Okay. You're right."

He gasped, smacked his hand across his forehead. "Excuse me, what did you say? Did I hear you say I was right?"

"I said, you're right. You are on occasion."

"Well, shut my mouth. I'll be damned. The woman said I was right." She smacked him on the shoulder as they headed back to the squad car.

Chief Baker was waiting in his office. Josh started down the hall, and the chief leaned out of his door, "Madison, I need to see you too."

Madison glanced over at Betty, who was standing behind the reception desk. Betty shrugged her shoulders and opened up her arms. Madison followed Josh down the hall.

"Close the door," the chief insisted.

"Madison, Josh, have a seat."

Madison took a long swallow and sat down without looking at Josh. She couldn't imagine what the chief was going to say. *Had someone reported Josh kissing my hand at the Breakfast Club?*

Josh undid his jacket and leaned back in the chair.

Chief Baker stretched back in this chair, "Madison, I know this has been your case, and I respect that. But it looks like we might have a murder on our hands and if so the Maitland Police Department has a crime to solve.

However, you and Josh work well together, and I would like you to continue with your investigation, but as part of our team. Do you have a problem with that?"

"When I accepted this case, it was to look for a mother's daughter. I didn't know what path this would take me down. Detective Logan has been instrumental in my investigation. I've been in law enforcement since I graduated from the FBI Academy. I have no misconceptions where a case like this one can lead. I want to bring closure to this family as much as you do. I have no problems following Detective Logan's lead on this."

The chief turned to Josh. "Josh, you have anything to add?"

"No, Sir, I think Agent Hart summed it up."

"Good, then you two find out who that body is in the back of that girl's car and who put it there."

Josh started for the door with Madison behind him. "Oh, and Agent Hart. Good to have you working with us again," the chief smiled.

"Thank you, Sir."

Josh headed for the door, but Madison hesitated to give Betty the thumbs up. Betty winked as Madison left.

"I don't know about you, but I sure could use a glass of wine, how about you?" Madison sighed.

"Sounds good. Where would you like to go?"

"I need to let Sophie out and feed her first. Why don't you drop me off at the office to get my car and I'll meet you at my place in about a half hour?"

"Okay."

"Why don't you pick up a pizza on your way over."

Josh looked puzzled. "Aren't we going out?"

"Would you rather go out or just unwind in a more relaxed atmosphere?" she winked.

He slumped slightly and chuckled. "And I thought you wanted to go out and party. I guess we can stay in if you want."

She leaned over and kissed him on the cheek and grinned.

He dropped her off in front of her office. Becca was still there. Madison opened the front door, and the bell rang, but Becca didn't come out. The light was on in the back room.

"I thought you would have gone home by now."

Becca was standing at the board, rearranging the leads, and timeline. "I just wanted everything to be up to date for you. Did you find anything in the car that would help us find Zoe?"

Madison hesitated and then stepped further into the room. "We're not sure, but there is a body in the back of the car."

Becca gasped for breath, "Was it Zoe?"

"We don't know yet. Dirt and cat litter covered the body."

"Cat litter?"

"Someone didn't want the decomposition of the body to smell and draw attention to the car. The entire car is at the lab. We won't know anything tonight. Why don't you go home and get some rest? I have a feeling we'll have a busy day tomorrow."

Becca sat down in the chair. "I had a bad feeling about this case."

"I know you did, and so do I, but we still have to follow the leads and investigate. Our job is just beginning, especially if the body is Zoe. I'll see you in the morning."

Becca put the dry-erase pen down and started out the door. "Okay, Boss. Have a good night."

"Thank you, Becca. You too. I'll ask Josh to bring us some coffee and donuts from Krispy Kreme in the morning. We're going to need more than bagels."

Becca just smiled. She grabbed her purse from her desk drawer and walked out of the office.

Madison stood in front of the board. What started out to be a young woman who may have been unhappy and left town, now might be a possible homicide. She sat down and then remembered Josh was coming over. She wanted to let Sophie out, feed her and take a shower before he arrived, so she closed up the office and drove home.

Sophie could hear her unlocking the door and rushed to greet her. The moment Madison opened the door, Sophie squeezed her little face between the door and wall to welcome Madison. "Hey girl, did you miss me today?" Sophie spun in circles and gave a little yap, then rushed to the French doors. "Okay, I'm coming."

Madison opened the doors, and Sophie sauntered out to the walled in yard. She sniffed around looking for that perfect place to do her business as though she had never been in the back yard before. Madison changed the water bowl and cut up some cooked chicken and frozen veggies and mixed them with Sophie's food.

As soon as Sophie came back in, Madison shut the doors and headed for the shower. Her body slumped under the hot pulsating water. Every muscle in her body was aching from the stress of the day, but the hot steaming shower helped relax her. When she finished, she put on her yoga pants and orange Gator hoody and plopped onto the couch.

She curled up and rested her head on the large purple and teal decorative pillow. She was finally relaxed and about to fall asleep.

KNOCK, KNOCK.

Madison bolted off the couch. Sophie was already at the door sniffing the threshold and wagging her tail. It had to be Josh. Sophie loved him and was always excited when he came over. "Who is that, girl?" she whispered. Sophie yelped one time. "Is that Josh?" She yelped again.

The moment she opened the door, Sophie started spinning in circles around his legs. "Someone in the house is always glad to see me." He put the pizza on the counter and leaned down and picked her up. Immediately, she licked him across the face. "You sure have some good sugar, little girl. I wish your momma were that excited to see me." He petted her head and then placed her back on the floor. Madison ran up to him, spun around and grabbed his face and gave him a big lick on his cheek.

"How's that?"

Josh burst out laughing. "I'm not sure that there aren't two bitches living in this house, and I mean that in a good way." He walked to the sink and pulled out a paper towel, dampened it and cleaned off his face.

Madison turned and faced Josh. "You're half right."

"What do you mean, I'm half right?"

"There is only one bitch in this house, and I'm that bitch. I'm so sorry."

"You have absolutely nothing to apologize for. I knew what I was getting into the first time I met you. I have always admired and respected you for your dedication to your job. I wouldn't have you any other way. I think that's what makes us such a great team. I don't want you to stop being the kick-ass investigator you've always been. I mean that, Maddy."

"I am a kick-ass investigator, Detective Logan. And don't you forget it.

Madison opened the pizza box and then pulled out two wine glasses from the cabinet. As she reached for the handle of the fridge to get the wine, Josh stepped in front of her, gently took her face in his hands and leaned into her. Then he licked her across her nose and grinned.

She laughed. "I had that one coming, didn't I?"

"You did."

He pulled her into his arms and kissed her. She returned his kisses, but these weren't the hot steamy kisses they had shared before. There was something different. She slightly pulled back and looked into his eyes. "I don't know why you put up with me, but I'm glad you do. I'm growing rather attached to you. I don't know what I'd do without you." Her eyes began to tear up. He kissed her eyelids. "Maddy, I've waited a long time for you to say that. You know how I feel about you. I have from the moment I saw you, in spite of your resistance to me. I just hoped, that in time, you would feel the same way."

She kissed him again. "We'd better have some wine and pizza, or I might get all mushy. You know, I'm not the mushy kind."

He smiled and watched her as she poured two glasses of wine. He served up two plates of pizza and carried them into the living room.

Chapter Seven

Madison awoke early, but Josh was still sleeping. She sat on the edge of the bed watching him and admiring his beautiful bare body. *How did I luck out with this man? He's good-looking, smart, a tough-as-nails detective, gentle, kind, and he cares for me. What took me so long to let him know how I felt? I could have lost the best thing that has come my way.* She leaned down and kissed him on the forehead and then slowly got out of bed.

Sophie was already waiting at the French doors to go outside. Madison pulled back the doors and left them wide open for the morning breeze, and then walked into the kitchen to start the coffee. This time, she was going to have it ready for him, not the other way around.

Josh was still sleeping so she poured a cup for herself and strolled out to the patio. There was light mist in the air from the evening rains, and it was still early enough that there was only silence and peace. The traffic hadn't started roaring on the highway yet, and people weren't coming in and out of their homes rushing to get to work. The only sounds were those of the mourning doves, the occasional echo of an owl through the trees and the whistle of the train in the far distance. It was her favorite time of the day. She held the steaming cup up to her face, closed her eyes and inhaled the aroma. Her body tingled as she reminisced about the evening with Josh and waking up with him lying next to her. She surrendered to the last few moments of peace. Soon she would be launched back into another homicide case, but for now she was calm.

She brought the hot cup to her lips and was about to take another sip of coffee when she felt the warmth of Josh's arms slid around her waist. He didn't say a word. He just held her in the quiet of the morning.

They stood drinking their coffee together. Josh gazed down at her. "How are you this morning? Are you ready to get down to business and solve this case?"

She blinked her eyes and crinkled her nose. "Speaking of work, would you mind buying Becca and us something to eat before you show up at the office? I kinda promised you would."

He waggled his eyebrows and winked. "No problem, Agent Hart. I'll see you shortly. You'd better get that beautiful body ready for work, or I might have another go at it."

She grinned as he walked to the door and left.

"One more cup of coffee, Sophie, and then I have to close the doors. I've got a crime to solve."

Madison wanted to study the board before anyone else arrived at the office. She finished her coffee, showered, dressed and grabbed her bag and rushed out the door. Becca would be showing up soon, and Josh would be arriving at the office shortly too.

She stepped up in front of the newly arranged board, thanks to Becca's eye for detail. What started out to be a mother trying to find her daughter had escalated into a murder case. But was the body that of Zoe McClain?

The bell at the front door rang. She looked down the hall to see Becca come in. "Good morning, Becca."

"Good morning, Boss."

The squeaky bottom drawer of Becca's desk open and closed. Becca had placed her purse in her desk and then walked down the hall to the case room. "Have you heard anything on the body yet?"

"No, it might take a while. Doc Webb is very thorough and won't give us any details until he's sure. I've tried on other cases to nag him into leaking some tidbit to me, but he's firm on his stance. Whoever it is, we still have a murder on our hands. That body didn't climb into the trunk of that car and cover itself with dirt and cat litter."

The front door opened again. "Hey, anybody here?" Josh yelled out.

Becca looked down the hall, and Josh was doing his juggling act trying to carry three coffees and a box of donuts. She turned to Madison, "He has donuts again." She winked at Madison. *Every time Josh spends the night with Madison; he brings donuts the next day.* "I hope you had a nice evening."

Madison turned her head, "What does that mean?"

"Oh, nothing. I was just hoping you got some rest after yesterday."

Madison suspected Becca knew Josh stayed over. *I guess the donut thing gives me away.* She smiled to herself. "I had a great evening, thank you."

Becca reached out and quickly took the coffees from Josh before he had a chance to spill them. Balancing coffee cups was not high on his list of accomplishments.

Madison started to lean over and kiss him and then drew back. She immediately glanced over at Becca, who had a Cheshire grin spread across her face. Madison just shook her head. "Okay, Becca, you can wipe that look off your face. Yes, Josh and I are seeing each other. There, are you satisfied? I said it."

Josh dropped his jaw to his chin. His heart nearly jumped from his chest. *She admitted that we're seeing each other.*

Madison reached for a donut and some coffee. "Now, can we get back to work, you two?"

Josh grabbed a donut and turned to Becca. Becca smiled and winked. "Sure thing, Boss."

"Yes, Ms. Hart," Josh smiled.

Madison stood studying the updates. "Okay, I think we all agree that Zoe McClain might be a victim of foul play, but we don't know if it is her body we found yesterday. Also, we have a few people of interest," she said pointing to the names across the top of the board. "Becca, today I'd like you to dig up all you can on Stephen Clark and Charlie Foster. We are now working with the Maitland Police Department on this case, so if you need any of their resources, I'm sure Josh can plug you into that to find what you need. You might want to check with Betty over there. She's good at locating information and between the two of you, I think we'll have what we need to either move them closer to the top or eliminate them. Josh, do you have anything to add?"

"Not really. I have a few unanswered questions, but I'm going to wait on that until we find out more on these guys. I'd like to go over to the lab this morning and see the car and how they are coming along with the evidence and removal of the body."

Madison took another sip of coffee. "I would too. The sooner we find out who our victim is, the sooner we can move forward. Of course if it is Zoe, we'll have to inform Denise McClain, and that is one part of this job I don't look forward to."

Josh took a chunk out of a powdered donut. He stood with one hand on his hip in front of the board with powder on his face, and down the front of his jacket. "I'd like to know if there were any other men Zoe met online or had in her life."

Madison bit her lower lip and looked away to keep from laughing. "You certainly wear those powdered donuts well."

He looked down at his jacket, then back at her standing there with her hand over her mouth. He dusted off his jacket. "There, is that better?"

Madison picked up a napkin and wiped his mouth. "You're so cute when you're angry."

"I'm not angry," he grunted. "I'm never bringing those donuts here again. From now on they'll be just plain generic cake donuts."

Madison smiled. "Ah, but you look so good in white."

"Becca, you're boss is a smart-ass, isn't she?"

"Don't pull me into this," she grinned.

Josh took the napkin from Madison and walked out of the room to the bathroom to make sure she got it all. By the time he returned, she was ready to go. "Doc should be in the lab by now. Are you ready?"

"I am if you're done picking on me."

Madison reached up and kissed him on the cheek and whispered, "I'm sorry, old habits die hard."

His face quickly softened, and his mood changed. "I don't want you to change. I wouldn't know how to react if you were sweet to me all the time. My suspicious nature would conjure up a plot. No, I love…I mean like you just the way you are."

"Let's go, Romeo," she joked.

They drove over to the coroner's lab. Zoe's car was in a garage area attached to the lab. When they arrived, Doc Webb and his assistant Joey were just beginning to sift through the dirt and cat litter. They painstakenly went through it cup-by-cup searching for anything that might be evidence.

Doc Webb stood about 5'6 ½" tall and never came to work without his bow-tie and a button- down freshly-ironed and starched dress shirt. He lowered his head and looked over his glasses."Good morning, Ms. Hart, Josh. What brings you two here so early?"

"We just wanted to see how the examination was going," Josh replied.

"Surely, you didn't think I'd have answers for you already, did you?"

"Of course," Madison replied.

"This is going to take some time. We have bodily fluids we're collecting from beneath the car and fingerprints have to be processed. Joey and I have to remove what's covering this body. Why don't you give me a call later in the day? We might be down to the body by then."

Madison walked around the car. The car doors were all opened. She donned her latex gloves and reached under the driver's seat.

Doc stood up and watched her leaning into the car."Ms. Hart, what are you looking for?"

"I just had a hunch. Sometimes women will put an extra small purse under their seat, so they don't have to lug a big bag around. I was checking to see if there was one here."

"Well?" Doc asked.

Josh walked up behind her. "Is there anything there?"

Madison pulled out a small artisan-crafted teal and green pouch, only big enough for money and maybe a credit card or two. "Yes, I did. Doc, did you find a larger purse in the car?"

"No, we did not."

She opened the pouch and found a receipt from a cable company dated a week before Zoe went missing. She placed it all into an evidence bag, zipped it closed and handed it to Josh. "This might be something we need to look into."

"No stone unturned, right?" Josh jested.

"That's right, Detective. You never know where even a minute clue will lead."

She sat down in the driver's seat, and could barely reach the gas peddle. "Doc, has anyone pulled this seat back?"

Doc put down his cup of dirt and walked over to the car. "How tall are you, Ms. Hart?"

"I'm about 5'4."

"I see, and yet you cannot reach the gas. How tall is your missing lady?"

"5'2." There is no way she drove this car."

Doc scratched his head. "I should say not."

Madison got out of the car and Josh got in. He comfortably could reach the gas.

Doc stepped up to the car door. "How tall are you, Josh?"

"I'm 6'2." The person who sat here last was at least as tall as I am, or he pushed back the seat to throw us off. I doubt that it would be our missing girl but anything is possible." But he didn't think Zoe was the last one behind the wheel, and neither did Madison.

"You're right about that, Detective. The last person who drove this car could have pushed the seat back to lead us in the wrong direction. Doc, did the forensic team dust the handle on the seat adjustment?"

"I'm not sure."

Josh called the station and discovered they had not dusted for prints on that spot yet. Josh had a kit in the back of the squad car. "I'll be right back. I've got to get my fingerprint kit."

"No need. I have one in the top drawer of my desk. Joey is studying forensic and likes to dust for prints throughout the lab."

Josh dusted for prints but there was only a partial, and it was too smudged to give any detail.

"Thanks, Doc. We'll give you a call later."

Doc and Joey returned to sifting through the trunk, and Madison and Josh headed back to the office to follow-up on the cable receipt.

Madison called the roommate. "Mr. Smith, this is Agent Hart. Can you tell if Zoe had cable installed in her room?"

"Yes, she did. She had it put in about two weeks before she moved, but that's all I know."

"Thank you." She hung up and turned to Josh. "Apparently, she just had it installed two weeks before she went missing. I'd like to talk to the company and find out who installed it and interview him."

"While you're doing that, I want to check into the online dating service she was using. I'll drop you off at the office. I have a few things to take care of at the station. How about if I come by later and pick you up for lunch?"

"Yeah, that sounds good. I want to see if Becca has anything for us."

On the way back to the office, Josh's cell phone rings. "Logan." Madison sat waiting for another response from him, but he said nothing. He hung up and turned the car around.

"What was that about?"

"That was Doc. They found something."

"A body?"

"He didn't say."

Madison could feel her pulse throbbing and a knot formed in her throat. The anticipation was killing her. She bit down on her lip so hard that she tasted the blood trickling in her mouth. A chill ran down her back, and that gut feeling hit her. *I know it's Zoe. I can feel it.*

Josh sped to the back of the lab and leaped out of the car, and Madison was close behind him.

"What do you have, Doc?"

Doc walked to the back of the car. They hadn't sifted through much more than when Josh and Madison left. But it was clear there was a blanket beneath the dirt. Doc and Joey continued dusting the dirt to the side as a figure of a body slowly emerged beneath the blanket.

Josh stood quietly as Doc gently pulled back the top of the blanket to reveal the torso of a body. "Whoever put this body in here tried to conceal it by twisting and bending it to squeeze into the small area in the back of this compact car. And they used some chemical that nearly disintegrated her clothing. I believe it's lye, but I won't confirm that until the lab runs an analysis on it."

The sweat was pouring off Madison's hands as she watched Doc and Joey continue revealing the body. They finally got close to the head. Someone had taken the time to put a scarf over her face before wrapping her in the blanket.

Josh took a long deep breath and gulped. "Well?"

Doc turned and looked at both of them. "I believe it's a female, but other than that I won't know until I do an autopsy how the cause of death or any other pertinent details. I wish I could tell you more, but it's still too soon."

Madison didn't have to know more; she knew who it was. Now, she needed to know why and who put her there. Her face turned red; she grit her teeth, and her hands turned into fists. She wanted the scumbag that did this.

Josh turned to her. "Let Doc do his job, so we can find out who our victim is." He gently guided her back towards the car. "Maddy, we'll get who did this, we always do, but until we have a positive ID, we cannot assume it's Zoe. I'm sure Doc will expedite this case. In the meantime, we need to stay focused on our end and do what we do best, investigate, right?"

"I hate this part of this job. I'm going to have to tell another mother that her daughter has been murdered?."

He put his arm around her and walked her to the car. She just sat there staring out the window as they drove off. Josh swung in the drive-through at McDonald's and ordered two black coffees.

She thought they were going back to the office, but Josh headed toward Lake Lily. He pulled up under a tree in the parking lot facing the lake. "Are you alright?"

"No, I'm not. Josh, I'm tired of finding dead bodies. I thought when I opened my Private Investigation Agency that I would land challenging cases, but why do they always involve murder? Maybe I should just advertise that I only do cheating spouses and missing money cases or something."

He reached his arm around the back of her seat. "Then who would speak for the dead? Madison, you have a gift, and you do it well. You are the voice of those who can no longer speak for themselves, and you bring them justice."

She dropped her head for a moment, and then looked into his eyes. "Thank you, I needed to hear that. Now, can I have that coffee?"

He softly smiled. "That's my Maddy. Let's have our coffee at our favorite table." They walked down to the table overlooking the lake.

Madison just sat watching the ducks playing along the shore, and the fountain in the middle of the lake. "I've told you the stories of my youth and spending our fourth of July's here, didn't I?"

"Yes, but you can tell me again."

"It just brings back such fond memories. I can remember my mother making the Chamber of Commerce float one year. She had bolts of white satin, and Dad built a frame that looked like a three-tiered cake. Then mother wrapped the fabric around each layer and decorated it to represent the birthday of America, and several neighborhood children got to ride on it. We were so proud of Mom. She was an amazing person. I don't know how she did what she did and still raise us kids."

A tear rolled down her cheek. Josh just leaned over and kissed her eyes. "You must have taken after your mother then because you are an amazing woman. Why do you think I waited so long for you?"

She reached up and stroked his face. "I sure wouldn't have waited for someone as bitchy as me."

"Ah, you're not *that* bitchy,"

"You didn't have to agree with me," she joked. "Enough mushy stuff. We need to get back to work."

Josh jumped up from the table and saluted her, "Yes, Agent Hart."

He took her empty coffee cup and tossed it in the trash as they walked back to the car. "Wow, I didn't think we were here that long, but it's almost time for Becca to go home. We'd better get over there and see if she's found anything on our cast of characters."

Madison chuckled. "I like that. Our cast of characters, and that they are."

They pulled up in front of the office, but Becca's car was gone. Madison furrowed her brow. "That's strange, she usually stays until I get back."

"She probably had something to do. I'm sure she'll call."

The door was locked, but the light was still on inside. Nothing looked disturbed or out of place. Madison just shook her head, and they proceeded to the case room. There was a note taped to the board. *Be back soon.* "I hate when I don't know what's going on," Madison grumbled.

"Maddy, she's a big girl, and I'm sure it must have been important. If it's related to the case, she will fill you in when she gets back."

"But she usually updates the board, and I don't see anything new up there."

"That's because there hasn't been anything new since we left, or at least anything new from our end."

"Right. We haven't talked to her since we found out Doc revealed a body. I guess I'm just eager to get to the bottom of this. I know this will sound odd, but I wish Doc had been able to tell us whether it was Zoe or not. I feel like I'm treading water right now. We can't say anything to her mother until we know for sure, and we can't proceed with our investigation into this homicide until we know who our victim is."

Josh took a deep breath. "This might be a good time for you to call it a day, go home, take a nice long, hot bath, have a glass of wine and go to bed."

"You're not coming over?"

Josh pulled her to his chest. "No, I think you could use a little time to yourself and get some rest. I'll see you in the morning. Now, please, get some rest. There's nothing else we can do until Doc informs us on the who and how."

She smiled up at him. "You're making me nervous. How did you start getting so smart when I seem to fall into a pit of uncertainty?"

"You just finally realized that you don't have to do it all alone," he grinned. "And it's about time."

Madison turned off the light and started for the front of the office. Just as she was about to close up for the night, Becca came in. "Are you two leaving?"

"We were, but not if you have something for us." Madison blurted.

Becca headed to the back room, flicked on the light and started on the board. "Well, I called Betty, over at the station, and she was more than helpful. We decided we could get more done if I went over there with her. She gave me access to the computer, with the permission of Chief Baker, and we did an in-depth search on our person's of interest."

Madison leaned forward onto the desk and Josh straddled the chair as they intently gave Becca their undivided attention. Josh gave Madison a quick glance with his head slightly cocked. This couldn't have come at a better time. Just another sign that Madison didn't have to do it all herself.

Becca stood tall at the board, "Okay, let's start with Stephen Clark. This guy has been in and out of mental institutions for schizophrenic episodes and delusional attachments. His delusion about his relationship with Zoe wasn't his first, and after confrontations with his other victims, he often displayed violent tendencies. He had been accused of stalking to the point that restraining orders were put out on him. Each time he insisted his victim wanted to see him again. But because of his diagnosis they returned him to the hospital instead of jail. So, I think he should remain at the top of our list of suspects in the disappearance of Zoe."

Madison stood up and crossed her arms. "Becca, I just might have to give you a raise. That's good work and saved me from a lot of running around."

Josh smiled. "Good work."

"Well, I couldn't have done it without Betty. She's amazing. I enjoyed working with her."

Madison took a deep breath, "Yes, good work. Now, let's call it a day and meet here early tomorrow and review what we have. Thank you, Becca," said said as she started for the door.

"Wait! That's not all."

Madison turned around to see Becca attack the board again, only this time she started scribbling under Charlie Foster's name. "Betty and I dug into Mr. Foster too. Since he's been on the job, there have been several burglaries in the complex. So we checked his work history and found the same thing happened at other apartments complexes where he worked. The robberies stopped once he was let go. I don't think that's a coincidence, do you?"

Madison jerked her head back, "No, I don't."

"But we could not find any incidences of violent behavior with Mr. Foster."

Becca sat down, lifted her head and crossed her arms, "That's what I've been doing today."

Josh snickered and bit his lower lip. "I think you've got a budding investigator in this office."

Madison smiled, "I believe you're right. Becca, I appreciate what you've done today. You have no idea how much this will help, but now I need you to quit for the day. I think we all could use a good night's sleep. I have a feeling this case is about to take us in a new direction." She didn't mention what she and Josh found out. She was tired and was ready to give in to Josh's suggestions for the night. "Josh, would you mind picking up some coffee and bagels, and let's all meet here in the morning? We'll update the board with any and all we know to this point and plan our next move."

Becca couldn't erase the smile off of her face. She lifted her chin, and with her shoulders back, she strutted out of the office.

Josh took Madison by the arm and boasted a big grin. "I don't want to be the one to say I told you so, but, I told you so. You're not alone in this, now get that pretty little ass of yours home before I weaken and chase you there."

Madison chuckled. "Oh no, far be it from you to rub it in my face." She reached up and kissed him on the cheek. "I'll see you in the morning." She turned and started to leave.

Josh gave her a slight smack on the butt. She flung around with her eyebrow raised, and her head cocked.

Josh lifted his hands in the air. "Too much?"

Madison did not respond, but turned and walked to her car. She wanted to be upset and normally she would have been outraged at that, but somehow coming from him she almost enjoyed it. But she wasn't going to let him know.

Josh stood there watching her drive home. He wanted to be with her, but his instincts told him she needed some time alone to digest what's going on. Madison wasn't the type of woman to push professionally or personally. When her car turned into the complex and disappeared, he drove home.

She opened the front door to a greeting little pup eager to see her. "Hey girl, did you miss me today?" Sophie did her usual spinning around and then raced to the French doors and waited for Madison to open them. "I'm coming, I'm coming."

Sophie bolted out the doors, and Madison headed to her bathroom to draw a bath. She poured in the lavender oils into the hot water, lit a few vanilla scented candles throughout the house and turned on some relaxing flute music, Cry of the Laughing Owl. She stripped off her clothes and put on her robe. By the time she came back to the kitchen for a glass of wine, Sophie was already curled back up on the couch. She poured a glass of wine and walked over to sit next to Sophie. "It's just you and me tonight." Sophie reached her tiny paws up to Madison's face and then snuggled her head close. Madison reached over to pet her. "I think my bath is ready," she whispered as she got up. Sophie bolted for the bedroom and jumped up on the bed. "You're a pretty smart pup."

She laid her robe on the bed, placed her glass of wine on the edge of the garden tub and then slid into the hot bubble bath.

Chapter Eight

Madison awoke in the middle of the night thinking about the case. She was eager to find out who's body it was in the trunk of that car. She was curious about the mound of dirt too. It looked like dirt she had seen before. *Could this be garden dirt used in landscaping?* She tried going back to sleep but ended up getting out of bed. She opened her home office area. "This is where my agency started. Amazing how much was done out of this small room." There was a small white board, a table, and two chairs. She vowed she wasn't going to bring her work home with her like she did when she was on cases with the FBI, but soon found herself scribbling what she knew onto the board.

She turned to Sophie lying on the floor just outside the doorway to the home office. "Okay, I am going to approach this with the assumption that the body is Zoe's. I know I shouldn't assume anything, but we will for now. Since the day after she was last seen, her car had been sitting in the airport's long-term parking. That gave the un-sub time to kill her, empty her apartment, find the dirt and cover her, and then get the car to the airport without anybody seeing him or her. That had to take some planning. So, we will assume it was all done late at night or early morning. Sophie, are you listening to me?"

Sophie lifted her head and wagged her tail.

"Good girl." She smiled.

"So our timeline could begin late Thursday night after the roommate left for his girlfriend's and ended sometime on Sunday morning."

Madison looked at her clock. She had been in there since 2:30 a.m. and it was now 7:30 a.m. She told Josh she would be at the office at 8:00 a.m. "Hey, girl, you should have let me know it was time to get ready."

Sophie raced to the back door to be let out. Madison opened the door and then hurried into the shower. She quickly dressed, put fresh water down for Sophie, closed the French doors, and dashed out the door.

She pulled into the parking spot in front of her office just as Becca drove up.

"Good morning, Boss."

"Good morning, Becca. I hope you're ready for a busy day. Doc Webb ought to have the identification on our body today, which means we're going to be hopping around here."

"I am."

No sooner did Becca get her purse into the bottom drawer of her desk and Madison turned on the light in the case room, did Josh come stumbling in the front door with the usual. Becca just shook her head as she opened the door and took the coffee from him. "She's already in the back."

"How is she feeling this morning?"

"She seems rested and ready to go."

"Good."

Becca followed him to the back with the coffee.

"Good morning, Ms. Hart."

She didn't even turn around. She was too busy updating the board herself with the questions that plagued her that morning. She scribbled the same information she did at home. "Good morning, Detective."

"You certainly look wide awake. How much coffee have you had this morning?"

"Just a few cups. I was up early going over some thoughts I had on the case and wanted to post them on the board before I forgot. I know we're going to have a busy day ahead but this will help establish our timeline." She turned around to see Josh and Becca standing there squinting at the board. "I know. Becca, you can rearrange the board later, but can you read what I wrote?"

Becca took a sip of her coffee. "I'll figure it out."

Josh walked up closer to the board. "Do you mind recapping for me what you just wrote down?"

She turned to him with her hands on her hips. "My writing isn't that bad...is it?"

"No. I just want to be sure I understand it correctly."

"We know that the last time Zoe was seen or heard from was the Thursday night before she was reported missing. And her car was parked at the airport on Friday evening, which means if that is Zoe in the trunk of her car, she was killed sometime between late Thursday night and Friday morning. That leaves the killer only a short window of opportunity to clean out her apartment. I think he, or she, did it late at night with fewer chances of anyone witnessing him."

"Yes, that makes sense to me, but aren't *we* getting ahead of yourself with assuming the body is Zoe's?" Josh asked.

"I know I said we shouldn't assume, and normally I wouldn't, but my gut is telling me this is our girl. If Doc is not swamped with other cases, he should be able to confirm the identity today."

Josh nodded his head. "He should, and as far as I know this case is his priority."

"I'd like to go back to the coroner's this morning and look over the car again."

"I would too, but I don't want Doc to think we're pressuring him."

Madison agreed. "I just want to look at the position of the seat again, and do a few adjustments. Also, I'd like to send a sample of the dirt to the FBI lab for analysis. I'll call my friend Agent Wells about it later. I have a hunch about that dirt, but the lab will give us a more concrete place of origin. Are you ready to get going?"

Josh put down his bagel and coffee cup. "Okay, but I doubt Doc has any more to tell us than he did last night."

Madison headed for the front. "Becca, if anything new comes in, call us right away."

"Will do, Boss."

Madison jumped into her car, and Josh stepped up to her window. "Are you sure you wouldn't rather have me drive? I'm feeling your mind is spinning with speculation."

She hesitated for a moment and then got out of her car and walked toward the squad car. "Are you starting to read my mind, too? I just can't stop thinking about how this poor young girl, excited about starting a new year with her students, suddenly disappears and was most likely murdered. By who and why?"

"That's what we're going to find out," Josh replied as he got into the driver's seat.

They arrived at the coroner just about the time Joey was coming out of the back door. "Good morning, Detective Logan, Ms. Hart. Wow, I didn't expect you to get here this quick. We just found out a few minutes ago."

Josh stood there for a moment scratching his head. "What are you talking about?"

"Didn't the Doc just call you?"

"No. What's going on?"

"Uh, I'd better not say before the Doc tells you or I could be in trouble. He's in the lab about to start the autopsy. We were able to remove the body from the car last night and.. I'd better keep my mouth shut and let him tell you."

Madison could see Joey was nervous. She smiled. "That's okay, Joey. We were on our way to see if there was anything new. We won't let him know you said anything."

"Thanks, Ms. Hart."

They walked past the car and headed down the hall to the lab, and Josh turned to Madison. "What do you think they found out?"

"Well, I'm hoping the identity of our victim."

As they entered the lab, Doc turned towards them, dressed in scrubs, a mask over his face and holding up a scalpel. "You certainly didn't waste any time. I just finished hanging up with your assistant telling her to have you two give me a call."

No sooner did he get his words out of his mouth, Madison's cell phone rang. It was Becca. She stepped over to the side of the room. "Yeah, Becca?"

"Doc Webb just called and said he had something important to tell you. I figured you had already heard, but in case you were sidetracked, I didn't want to take the chance."

"Josh and I are here now. I'll get back to you. Thank you."

Madison walked back to the table where Doc Webb was beginning his autopsy.

He smiled at Madison. "I take it that was your assistant, Becca Hamilton?"

"Yes, she was just telling me you called."

"Is that Sandra Hamilton's daughter?"

"It is."

"I knew her parents. Nice people. I used to play golf with her father at Dubsdread Country Club. Oh, that was so long ago. How's she doing?"

Josh began to fidget but didn't want to interrupt him. Madison was also eager to hear what the Doc learned.

"She's doing fine and is a great help. She mentioned you wanted to tell us something?"

"Oh, yes. I took an impression of our victims teeth and sent them off early this morning and just received a reply," he said as he leaned over the body to make another cut.

"And?" Josh asked.

"Yes, your victim is Zoe McClain."

Josh took a deep breath. "Thank you, Doc."

He and Madison turned to leave. Just as they were about to walk out, Doc hollered out, "That's not all."

Madison swung her head around and widened her eyes. "What else did you find?"

Doc put his scalpel down, reached over to a dish on his tray and picked up something. "Looks like your victim was shot with a 22-Caliber in the back of the head."

Madison and Josh turned to each other and were just about to bolt out of the door when Doc Webb hollered again. "She was shot three times in the head. You're the investigators, but it looks like over-kill to me. If I find anything else after my autopsy, I'll let you know."

Josh walked over, picked up the shell and then bagged it. "Thank you, Doc."

"One more thing before you leave. She was shot at close range, all three times."

Madison shook her head and followed Josh out to the car. They immediately took the shell to the forensic lab to have it analyzed and tagged as evidence. "I think we need to update the Chief before we make our next move."

Madison leaned her head against the back of the seat. "Yeah, then I need to see Mrs. McClain."

"Don't you want to know all the facts before you talk to her?"

"What more does she need to know, other than her daughter is dead. Looks like it was a sudden death, and that's all I'll tell her if she asks."

Josh put his arm around the back of her seat. "Do you want me to go with you?"

"No. She hired me to find her daughter. I think this is something I need to do on my own. Just drop me off at the office so I can get my car."

"Okay."

Josh parked his car next to Madison's at the office, expecting she would come in first and update Becca. Instead, she reached for the door handle.

"Aren't you coming in first?"

"I need to deal with this now. You can update Becca. I'll call you later."

Josh stood next to his car as she backed out and headed toward Horatio Avenue. As soon as she was out-of-sight, he opened the office door. Becca was sitting at her desk.

"Where is Ms. Hart going?"

"Let's go back to the case room and get the board updated. If I know Maddy, she's going to want to hit this case running when she gets back. I'll fill you in back there."

Josh picked up some of the papers on the missing, now dead girl, and looked over at the board.

"Detective? Was it Zoe'?"

"It was, and that's why Madison left. She's on her way to notify Zoe's mother. I sure don't envy her. I've been in her shoes too many times in my career, and it never is easy telling the family that their loved one has been murdered."

Becca lowered her head. She sniffled slightly and then stood tall. "What can I do?"

"Do what you do best, have everything ready for her when she gets back. I know from this point on, Madison is going to be like a bulldog with a bone. And she won't let go until she catches the bastard who murdered this young lady."

"I hate to ask, but was Ms. McClain violated, you know, was she raped?"

"We don't know, but by the looks of it, she was caught off guard."

"How do you know that?"

"I don't, but three shots at close range usually indicates that someone snuck up on the victim and killed them."

"How awful, but at least Madison won't have to tell the mother that her daughter had been raped. It's bad enough she's dead, but if I was a mother and my daughter had been killed, I'd pray it was quick with no pain."

"It seems that's what happened, but that won't keep Madison from hunting him or her down."

Becca looked up at Josh, trying to hold back her tears. This was the first homicide case that Becca had been involved with of someone so young and innocent. "I know you both will catch who did this."

Josh slammed the papers down on the table. "You're damn right we will."

✂

Madison slowly drove down Highway 17-92 towards Altamonte Springs. Denise McClain lived about fifteen minutes away, but Madison took her time. She turned onto Seminole Blvd and headed east to Lake Drive. She sipped her cold coffee and swallowed hard. She saw the McClain home just up ahead on the left. The closer she got, the more nervous she became. This was her first independent assignment, and she was about to inform the mother who wanted to find out where her daughter was that she was dead.

Denise was outside watering her rose garden when Madison pulled up in the driveway. Madison had never been to the McClain home before. Most of their conversation had been at the office or on the phone. Madison opened the car door and started walking up to her. Denise dropped the hose and fell to her knees. Madison raced to her and knelt down beside her.

Madison held Denise by the arm to steady her. Denise lifted her head with tears flooding down her face. "You found my daughter. She's dead, isn't she?"

Madison helped Denise up and escorted her into the house and onto the couch. "Can I get you some water?" Denise couldn't respond. Madison walked into the kitchen and poured a glass of cold water and returned to the distraught woman.

She sat down next to Zoe's mother and put her arm around her shoulder. Madison bowed her head slightly, her eyes welled up with tears and a hard lump formed in her throat. "Yes, we found her. I'm so sorry."

Denise fell against Madison's chest, and she wept. After a few moments, she leaned back reached up and held Madison's face and looked her into her eyes. "You'll tell me the truth, won't you. Did she suffer?"

Madison held their eye contact and took a hold of Denise's hands. "No, she did not suffer." Madison couldn't say anything else; her voice began to crack. Denise forced a slight smile, "Thank you for that."

"Denise, is there someone who can come and stay with you for awhile?"

"My sister lives down the street. I guess I'd better call her. Would you mind staying here until she can come over?"

"Not at all. I'll stay here as long as you need."

Denise tried to get her cell phone out of her purse, but her hands were shaking too much. "Would you mind, Ms. Hart?"

Madison reached in and pulled out the cell phone, and tried to hand it to Denise. She started shaking again, almost uncontrollably. Madison reached for the phone. "What is your sister's name?"

"Margaret."

"What's Margaret's last name?"

"Margaret Young."

Madison did a search and found Margaret Young's number. She dialed it and then handed the phone to Denise. Someone answered, but all Denise could do was weep. Madison took the phone. "Is this Margaret Young?"

"Yes, it is. Why are you answering my sister's phone?"

"Ms. Young, your sister asked me to call."

"Is Denise alright?"

"Yes, but she needs you right now."

"Oh dear God, they found Zoe, didn't they?"

"Can you come over now?"

"I'm on my way." And she hung up.

Denise could barely speak. "Thank you, Ms. Hart."

Madison just sat with her. Within five minutes, Margaret came flying through the door and rushed to Denise. Margaret threw her arms around her sister, and they wept. Denise leaned back, "It's Zoe', she's gone."

Madison sat across the room and waited until she thought it was time for her to leave. "Denise, is there anything else I can do for you right now?"

"Find who hurt my Zoe."

"I will!"

Margaret walked Madison to the door. "Thank you, Ms. Hart."

"I wish I didn't have to bring this news."

"As much as my sister wanted to hold onto hope, I think she knew something had happened to Zoe. Zoe would have called her mom by now."

When Madison got back into her car, she slumped over the steering wheel and wept. Suddenly she sat up, wiped her eyes, gritted her teeth and backed out of the driveway. "I'm coming for you, you bastard!"

Chapter Nine

Madison sped down the highway. The veins in her neck were throbbing. She had a death grip on the steering wheel, and her knuckles were turning white. All she could think about was finding who was responsible for taking this young woman's life.

Her car finally came to a screeching halt in front of her office. She dashed through the door and raced to the back. Josh was sitting watching Becca rearrange the board. He jumped up when she flew into the room; Becca nearly dropped the marker. "Are you alright?" Josh asked.

"No, I'm not. I had to tell a mother that she was never going to see her daughter again. I'm going to nail this bastards ass to the wall."

Cautiously he opened his mouth. "Okay...then. I think we'd better get to work. I just got a call from Doc Webb. He said there were no signs of sexual assault. So we can rule out rape."

It was nearly 5:30 p.m. and they had been at it most of the day. Madison was exhausted but didn't want to stop. Her old bulldog mode was kicking into gear. However, Josh suggested they take a break and hit it fresh in the morning. "Why don't we all break for the day? Tomorrow, you and I can go back to the lab and check out the car again, and maybe we'll hear something from your friends at Quantico about the soil samples."

All Madison could do was stare at the board. She rooted herself in one spot with her hands on her hips scanning back and forth at the people of interest, the timeline and then back at the table. Then she picked up a few of the unknown bits of papers they found in Zoe's trash. "There has got to be a connection here. What is this board *not* telling us?"

Becca turned to Josh and then to Madison. "Boss, if you don't need me anymore this evening, I'll see you in the morning."

Madison didn't move. Josh stepped up and tapped her on the shoulder. "Madison."

"Uh?"

"Becca is leaving."

"Oh, yeah. Thank you for updating the board, Becca. I'll see you in the morning."

Becca lowered her head and slowly walked to her desk. She sat there waiting just a little longer in case Madison needed something, but there was only silence, so she pulled her purse out of the bottom drawer and left.

Josh heard the front door close. "Maddy, I know you're upset, and I want to get the person as bad as you do, but neither of us is going to be any good if we don't get some rest. You always do better when you're fresh. Let me take you home."

"Josh, if you could have seen the anguish on that mother's face when I told her Zoe was dead. I felt her pain. I could barely hold myself together. I never want to bring children into this world and suffer a loss like that. We have got to find this person before he takes another loved one away from their family."

"We will, but not tonight." He turned her around, away from the board. "Please, for the sake of the case, go home and get some rest. I need you to be at the top of your game tomorrow so we can do our job."

"You're right. I hate it when you're right," she softly smiled. "But you don't have to take me, I'll be alright."

"Are you sure?"

"Yes, I just needed to vent. I promise I'll go home and curl up with Sophie and get a good nights sleep." She looked up at him and smiled. "Will you bring the coffee and bagels?"

"I'll be here bright and early."

She stepped up closer and kissed him. "Thank you."

Josh smiled, returned a kiss and then motioned her out of the room, turned off the light and followed her to the front. He was going to make sure she had left before he drove off. He locked the door behind her, and then she got in her car, waved and drove home. Josh stood next to his car and watched as she turned into her complex. He wanted to run by and talk to Doc Webb one more time before he called it a day but didn't want her to know.

He pulled into the parking lot at the lab. There were no lights on, so he drove around to the back and saw a light coming from the garage where Zoe's car was being processed. The only people still there were Doc Webb and Joey. They were still sifting through each cup full of dirt and placing it on a large tarp spread on the floor. They had arranged the dirt on the tarp to replicate where it was found in the car. "Doc, could you use an extra hand?"

"Thank you, Detective. That would be nice. I need to send this young lad home. He's been here since early this morning, and I'm afraid he's going to fall asleep."

"I not tired, Doc. I was just adjusting my eyes."

"Joey, go home. Detective Logan can give me a hand. I'll see you in the morning. Now, go," Doc insisted.

"Are you sure?"

"I'm sure."

"Good night Doc, good night Detective."

Josh nodded. "Good night Joey."

Doc Webb stretched his back and shrugged his shoulders as he watched to make sure Joey left. He whispered. "Josh, how's the case going?"

"We don't have enough evidence to pursue a lead. So far, everything appears to be a dead end. I was hoping to find something new here, so Madison and I had a direction to follow tomorrow."

"How is Ms. Hart?"

"I think this case is hitting her harder than the others. She spent time with the victim's mother today and that didn't go well. I'm afraid she's going to drive herself too hard."

"Yes, I understand. She just called here a few minutes before you arrived to find out if we had discovered anything new."

Josh dropped his head. "Damn, I was hoping she'd go home and relax."

"She been doing this type of work a long time. It's in her blood, and I don't suppose she's going to change now. She'll be all right. You two make a good team, and I have no doubt you will find the perpetrator of this crime too. But, you are also a driven man. I've seen you spend sleepless nights over a case. I'll bet she doesn't know you're here, does she?"

"No, and I'd rather she didn't." Josh picked up a small spade and started sifting through the dirt.

After about an hour of sifting through the dirt, Doc lifted his head. "Well, what do we have here? I think the forensic team will be interested in this."

Josh walked over, picked up a small button that appeared to have come off of a shirt or blouse. He bagged and tagged it and put it in his pocket. "I'll have it sent to the lab. It could have already been in the dirt, or it could have come from our killer, but we'll take all the pieces we can. Sometimes they fit just perfectly into the puzzle."

Doc gave a big yawn and stretched his back. "I think we both need to go home and rest."

"Yeah, you're probably right. I need to feel alert in the morning. See you later, Doc, and thanks for letting me help."

"Anytime, Josh."

Chapter Ten

Madison tossed and turned all night, reliving the vision of Zoe's distraught mother and wondering how many loved ones had suffered the same anguish. In all the years with the FBI, her focus had been on the perpetrators. It was someone else's job to notify the families. Now, working cases as a P.I, she was faced with all of that. *I'm not sure I'm ever going to get used to this. How does Josh do it?* She looked at the clock next to the bed; it was only 3:00 a.m., but there was no more fighting to go to sleep. She inched out of bed so she wouldn't disturb Sophie, walked into the kitchen and started the coffee. She stepped in front of the bi-fold door leading to her home office. "Should I?"

The whole reason for having an office down the street was so she would not bring her work home with her, but she was angry and eager to find who committed this crime. She grabbed the knobs on the doors and opened the room. The small whiteboard with the data she had put up the day before was glaring at her, but it was incomplete and gave little or no more clues as to how to proceed with this case. She had interviewed three people of interest with nothing jumping out to indicate they had anything to do with Zoe's murder. She paced back and forth in front of the board. "This is insane. I'm not going to learn anything here." She closed the doors and went for that first cup of coffee. She glanced at the kitchen clock; it was already 4:30 a.m.

She strolled to the French doors and opened them. It was still dark outside. She stepped onto the patio with her hot cup of coffee and breathed in the mist of the early hours. She closed her eyes, breathed again, but all she could see was the tear stained face of Denise McClain. Just then, she felt something against her leg. Sophie had quietly joined her. "Good morning, girl" She reached down and petted her. Sophie was quick to return a snuggle into her hand, and then she rushed out into the yard to do her morning ritual.

Madison headed back for a second cup of coffee. "I might as well get ready and head down to the office. I'm not going to get much done here." She hurriedly showered, dressed and pulled her papers together. She poured a large mug of coffee, closed the back doors and left.

She drove out of the complex. Not a single light was on in any of the townhouses, nor were there any cars on the street while she drove to the office. Normally the activity in town would bustle with people racing to go nowhere fast. Cars would be honking as they sped to their locations. The lights of the cafés would be blinking and headlights would flood the roads. But at that hour it was like a ghost town; silent, dead of activity and stillness that could conjure up all sort of stories. She pulled into the driveway, opened the office, turned on the light and went straight to the back room.

She shuffled through a few receipts she remembered from the day before. She sat down with her coffee reading the bits of papers found in the trash outside of Zoe's apartment.

Madison marveled at how well Becca had reorganized the board. A visual timeline began to emerge with each person of interest, and where they were during the times Zoe went missing. Unfortunately, they all had airtight alibis. She shook her head, sipping her coffee while scanning the board. "We're missing something or someone." She set her coffee on the table and walked up closer to the board, and stood there with her hands on her hips going over what they had. She scratched her head. "We have David George, who claimed to be a good friend, yet he's an ex-boyfriend; Stephen Clark, the strange character who thinks he and Zoe were in love, yet she never met him in person. He stalked her, but could he have killed her? Then we have Charlie Foster, the maintenance man. He had opportunity and means and he did possess some of the items belonging to our victim, but would he so blatantly display them if he had murdered her? We have the roommate, but he was with his girlfriend the entire weekend. However, the girlfriend could have snuck out while he was sleeping, but then she would have had to have help carting off all Zoe's belonging."

She rummaged through the receipts again. "Oh, yes. We haven't interviewed the guy who installed her cable the week before she went missing. He may be able to shed some light. Damn, I wish it were daylight, I'm ready to move on this."

She turned up her coffee mug and took the last gulp of the now cold coffee. It was 6:30 a.m. "I can't wait for Josh to bring more coffee, I need some now, and I know McDonalds is open. She left her bag on the table and grabbed her purse and headed out. McDonalds was right around the corner. She pulled into the drive-through and ordered a large black coffee and a sausage biscuit, something she rarely ate, but her stomach was growling. She headed back to the office. She opened the door, and there was Becca sitting at her desk. "What are you doing here this early?"

"Working. Good morning, Boss."

"Becca, it's not even 7:00 a.m."

"I know, but this case had me up most of the night. I couldn't sleep, so I thought I might as well be here as sitting on the couch waiting to be here."

"Would you like me to get you some coffee?"

"No, I just swung by McDonalds and got me a large coffee. This will be fine until Detective Logan comes." She smiled. "What are you doing here so early?"

"I couldn't sleep either. We make a great team, don't we?" she chuckled."

Becca picked up her coffee and followed Madison to the back. "Have you heard anything new?"

"Not really, I called Doc Webb last night to see if he had news, but he and Joey were still sifting through the dirt. We sent the sample of dirt to the bureau, but I'm sure that will take awhile. Our case is not on their priority list. It is more of a favor, however, they have a broader file to compare with and access to worldwide samples.

"Have you talked to Detective Logan since last night?"

"No. When I left here, he said he was going home to get some rest. I suspect he'll be here early this morning too. If I know him, he's going to be eager to get going on this investigate, and Chief Baker has given him the go-ahead to make this a major crime case."

"Well, I'm sure you two will solve this murder. You two seem to have the right chemistry for solving mysteries."

Madison took a big sip of her coffee. "Yeah, we do. Thanks for the reminder."

Becca stood looking at the board. "What's our next move?"

Madison liked hearing her enthusiasm. "*We* are going to interview the man who installed Zoe's cable, and hopefully, Doc will have something for us. He said he hoped to complete the autopsy today. I would like you to get with Betty again and see what you can find in Zoe's school computer. She may have some personal information in there that could help us understand the type of person she was and who she chatted with. See if she ever logged into her email from her school computer and if she did, who did she chat with."

"I'm on it."

"Hey, can I get a hand here," Josh hollered from the front door. He had his foot wedged against the door trying to push it open while doing his juggling act with the coffees. Becca darted to the front, pushed the door open the rest of the way and grabbed the box of coffee cups from him.

"What would we do without you, Becca."

Becca just shook her head. "Detective Logan, if I weren't here to help you, you'd only have to worry about two cups."

"Oh, yeah. How's Ms. Hart this morning?"

Madison stuck her head out into the hall, "Ms. Hart is doing great. How is Detective Logan doing?" she laughed.

"Ready to get to work."

He and Becca walked to the back. There were two large empty coffee cups on the table. "I see you started without me," he grinned. "You two must have gotten her before the sun came up."

Madison raised one eyebrow and grinned. "As a matter-of-fact, we did. I was thinking you and I could interview the cable guy."

"That's funny, the cable guy?"

"I was going over the receipts and saw that he had installed her cable a few weeks before she was murdered. She might have said something to him, or he may have seen, something that appeared out of the ordinary."

"Okay. And I'd like to stop by the lab and drop off this button."

"Where did you get that?"

"On the way home last night, I stopped by and visited with Doc while he was sifting through the dirt, and he found this. It may be nothing, but right now it's all we have."

"Detective Logan, I thought we agreed we were both going home last night to rest."

He shrugged his shoulders. "It was on my way."

Madison cocked her head and crossed her arms. "On your way? The lab is on the opposite side of town from your place. Did you get lost?"

He picked up his coffee and took a swig, trying to avoid eye contact with her. "I thought you'd be glad I found a clue, and besides, if I had mentioned I was going to stop there, you would have wanted to tag along."

"Tag along?"

"I didn't mean it like that. What I meant to say was I wanted you to be able to get some rest. I knew we would be stomping the ground for leads today."

Becca bit her lower lip. "I think I'd better get back to my desk. Thank you for the coffee and bagels, Detective."

"You're welcome.

When Becca was out of the room, Madison walked up as close as she could in front of him and whispered, "I know you were looking out for me, but this ain't my first rodeo, and I'm still your partner on this case. So don't leave me out of the loop, get it, Logan?"

He looked into her eyes, "I get it, but you sure are sexy when you're mad."

She smacked him on the shoulder. "I'm serious, Josh. Don't treat me like I'm frail, okay?"

He reached his arms around her. "I'm sorry. I don't think you're frail, nor do I think you cannot handle anything thrown your way, but even the toughest investigators need to step back, rest and regroup occasionally. After all you went through yesterday, it couldn't hurt for you to do the same. How do you think I deal with telling loved ones that their family member had been killed time after time. No one is immune to that. It hits hard. There have been many times after informing the loved ones, I have had to regroup, but then I kick-ass and get the bad guy. I wanted you to have the same opportunity."

It's so hard for me to let go, but I know he's right. She put her hands to his face, reached up and kissed him. "Thank you. Now, can we get to work?"

"That's my Maddy, to the point and ready to attack the case."

"After we interview the cable guy, I'd like to go over the car again. I have a hunch." She grabbed a bagel and her coffee and started down the hall to the front. "Becca, don't forget what we talked about. If something else comes up, call me."

"You've got it, Boss."

Josh was right behind her with a big grin on his face. When he passed Becca's desk, he turned and winked at her. She nodded her head and smiled.

Josh got in on the passenger's side of her car. There was no asking her if she wanted to take the squad car, she had her mind made up. "Would you run by the lab first, so I can drop off this button? I'll just run in. It won't take but a minute, you don't even have to turn the car off."

"No problem."

She pulled up close to the back door of the lab and Josh jumped out. She sat in the car going over the interviews they had done, trying to find something that stood out, but nothing came to mind.

Josh jumped back into the car. "Okay let's go."

"That didn't take long."

"I told you I was just going to drop it off. Now, let's talk to the cable guy," he snickered.

She raised one eyebrow and laughed. "You're not going to let it go, are you?"

"What are you talking about?"

"The cable guy thing."

He didn't respond. He took a big gulp of his cold coffee. "I could use a hot cup of coffee before we tackle that interview."

She sped out of the driveway and headed straight for the drive-through and ordered two large black coffees. "Now, are you settled? Do you need to go to the bathroom or need another donut before we get to work?"

He tilted his head and furrowed his brow. "I think I'm okay," he chuckled.

"Good."

They called the cable company and found out who had installed Zoe's cable. He was on an installation across town. Madison set her GPS. When they arrived, a man was loading up his equipment into the back of his van.

They pulled up behind him and approached. Josh looked inside the van. "Nice van, is it yours?" Josh looked at the man's name tag. It read Chris Adams. He was the man they were looking for.

The man glanced sideways and shut the door of the van. "Can I help you?"

Josh showed his badge and introduced himself and Madison.

"No, it's a company van. Why?"

"No reason. I'm just admiring the size. I need one about that size to move a few things this weekend."

"Well, my boss doesn't let us lend them out."

Madison stepped up and interjected herself into the conversation and handed him a receipt. "Did you do an installation at this address?"

"Yeah, Zoe McClain's place."

"You remember her name?"

"Of course. I met her while I was installing her cable. We went out a couple of times. What's this about?"

Josh kept looking at the van and then back at him. "How long did you two date?"

"Not that long. She wasn't really my type."

Josh unbuttoned his jacket and stood with his hands on his hips. "What is your type, Mr. Adams?"

"I just wanted to have a good time, but she wanted something more permanent. I think the chick was looking for a committed relationship. That's not for me. I had to dump her."

Madison wanted to punch him. "You dumped her?"

"Yeah."

"When did you *dump* her?"

"I don't remember. Like I said we only went out twice right after I installed her cable. She kept calling me and leaving me messages, but I didn't call her back. I haven't seen her since."

Josh took a deep breath, "Do you mind if I listen to the *chick's* messages? It might give us a better idea the state of mind she was in."

"I deleted them. Listen, I only went out with her a couple of times. I haven't talked to her or seen her since. Do you mind, I have another installation to do, and I need to get going."

Madison forced a smile. "No, we're done, for now. But we might need to talk to you again."

———⟶———

They stood as the guy finished loading up his things and drove off. Josh turned to Madison. "He could easily haul a lot in that van."

"He could, but he didn't seem that nervous with our questions, but I still would like to check him out. Josh, I feel like we're hitting a brick wall with this case."

"With each case we do, we hit that wall, and then something breaks through. We still have lots to check out."

Madison sat for a moment. "I want to go back to where it all started. Let's check out her apartment, only this time I'd like the forensic team to meet us there."

"Are you thinking she was murdered there and then transported?"

"Yes, I do. I'll call the roommate and let him know we're coming. I'm getting hungry, let's grab a bite to eat first."

"Sounds good. I'm getting sick of eating bagels every day for breakfast."

Madison chuckled. "Okay."

She pulled into a little restaurant on the way to Zoe's. There was a maroon awning hanging over the front door that read, Paul's. It looked like a mom and pop place. She hated eating at fast food places with the vision that her food had been waiting for her resting under a light for who knows how long. She liked seeing a cook preparing her food.

A young girl approached the table. She looked like she was still attending school. She was wearing a long, print skirt and a modest pale blue blouse. "Good morning," she said in a soft sweet voice. "Can I get you anything to drink?"

"I'll have some ice-tea," Madison replied.

"Just water for me," Josh answered.

She placed the menus on the table and returned to the end of the counter to get their drinks. Just as she set the drinks down on the table, the man at the grill hollered out something to her in a foreign language, and she answered him.

Madison looked up and smiled. "Is that your father?"

"Yes. This is our place. My mother works here too." She pulled out her tablet. "Have you decided what you'd like?"

Madison was still looking over the menu when Josh jumped in. "I'd like the Greek salad with chicken."

Madison asked, "What's in the Paul's Special Salad?"

The young girl smiled. "It has everything. My dad puts bacon, ham, chicken, hardboiled eggs, our home-grown tomatoes, and onions if you like them. And we serve it with warm pita bread."

Madison handed the young girl the menu. "I'll have that, please."

Madison took a sip of her ice tea and shook her head. "Such a sweet innocent young girl. It makes me cringe to think beyond those doors lie crazy people that would think nothing of taking a young girl's life. It's a sad world."

"Maddy, most people will never encounter in their lives what we do. We see the worse, but there is a lot of good out there."

She leaned back in her chair. "You're right. Sometimes it's just hard for me to see it, especially when we work cases like this one."

The young girl came out with two salads that each could have fed a family of four. Madison's eyes widened. "That looks great!"

"My father makes the best salads in town. I hope you'll like it."

Madison watched as the young girl returned to the counter. Her father nodded and waved at her and Josh. Not something you'd see in a fast food place.

"I'm afraid I won't be able to eat all of this in one sitting."

Josh dug into his like he hadn't eaten in a week. "Well, I will."

Madison laughed. "Somehow I got the feeling you would?" She ate as much as she could, and there was still plenty left on her plate, enough for another meal. She sipped on her ice-tea as Josh continued.

She kept glancing at the TV mounted above the counter. The news came on, and then suddenly she heard "The young woman who was missing has been found murdered." She jerked her head up. The report was about Zoe. She leaned across the table and grabbed Josh by the arm. His salad flung from his fork as he turned to see what she was talking about. "Is that about Zoe?"

"Ssshhh, yes. Good grief that was fast. I didn't even have time to tell Winter. I know she'll want the full story. I'll have to call Jim when we get out of here. Hurry and finish your salad."

"I'm done. I can take the rest with me."

Madison called the young girl over and asked for the check and a couple of to-go boxes. The girl pulled up the plates. Within moments, she returned with the boxed up salads, and the bill.

Madison grabbed the bag, "Josh can you get this, I've got to call Jim right away?"

"Sure."

Madison darted out of the restaurant and called the Sentinel. "Jim, this is Madison."

"Good to hear from you. How are things going?"

"That's the reason I called. I know you've heard about the body found at the airport."

"As a matter of fact, I did. What do you know about it?"

"It is in connection with a missing person's case I was working. That's why I called you. If you'll have Winter give me a call, I can fill her in on the all the details leading up to this point. The Maitland Police Department has asked me to help in the investigation into the murder. I can't give you any more information right now, but as I can, I'll relay our findings to Winter. That way she'll have the story ready to break when we can release it."

"Thank you, Madison. I'll have her call you today. I appreciate the heads up and the exclusive on this. I know if you're involved you'll find the suspect and bring justice to the victim. Take care and stay in touch."

"I will. Give my best to Jessie, and tell her to come by sometime."

"Will do."

Josh stepped outside carrying the boxes of leftovers. "Did you get a hold of Jim?"

"I did. Winter is going to call me later, and I'll fill her in on what we know so far."

"How much detail are you going to reveal to her? This is an ongoing case, and you know what that means."

"I also know my sister, Winter. She will write the story as we give her information, and when we can inform the press, she'll have the story ready to run with it. You don't have to worry about her. She's won't leak a thing. I just want her to have the story completed with the right facts."

"Yeah, I've read her last articles on the cases we've done. She's a damn good reporter."

Madison smiled. "That's my Sis. Now, we need to get moving on this. Let's go back to Zoe's apartment."

They started down Highway17-92 and Josh's cell phone rang. It was Betty. "Hey, beautiful. What's up?"

"You and Madison might want to swing by here. Calls are coming in on your case. I guess news travels fast when a crime is featured on TV. I've talked to the Chief. He wants the both of you to come in as soon as possible. How soon can you get here?"

"We're on our way."

Madison crinkled her nose and turned to Josh. "What was that all about? You didn't say much."

"It seems that story on TV about the body at the airport has generated a few calls and the Chief wants to talk to us about it."

They pulled into the back of the Police Station and entered through the back door. Betty spotted them in the hall and hollered out, "He's waiting for you in the conference room."

They walked past Josh's office to a large room on the right of the hall. Chief Baker stood up when they entered the room. "It seems calls are streaming in with people thinking they know something about the case. Too many for Betty to reply to alone. Madison, I was wondering if we could use Ms. Hamilton in this case."

"I'll ask her, but I'm sure she'll help. What do you need her to do?"

Chief Baker stood with his hands on his hips. "Betty tells me Becca is really good at organizing the facts. I was hoping that between her and Betty, they could screen some of the calls and redirect the ones that sound promising to you and Josh to follow up. Betty has a pile of papers on her desk with the information that's coming in. If Becca could assist her, we could address these calls as soon as possible. I can tell you that with the news release of this find that we are bound to get every quack coming out of the woodwork, but someone may have seen or heard something that will be crucial."

"We'll head back to my office as soon as we leave here. I'll talk to Becca and get right back to you."

Josh and Madison entered the reception area, and Betty handed them the stack of the incoming calls. They rushed out the back door and sped off to the office.

Madison swung open the door. Becca was in the back room. She had set up another smaller white board. "What's this?" Madison asked.

"Betty already called me. I know what you're going to ask me, and yes, of course, I'll help. I bought this extra board to keep the leads from the calls separate from our case board. That way we can eliminate the prank ones without destroying our case board."

Madison sat down at the table and looked at Josh. Josh gave a big Cheshire grin. "I'm afraid your assistant is going to be getting that raise."

Madison shook her head. "And a promotion."

Becca seemed focused on what she was doing and did not respond to either of them. She leaned down and picked up the pile of calls that Betty sent over. "I'll have these up right away. I took the liberty of asking Betty to reroute the calls over here so I can organize them without wasting time going back and forth to the station. I hope you don't mind. I just thought you two have enough on your plate with your investigation."

Madison walked over to Becca, put her hand on her shoulder and smiled. "If the Chief tries to steal you from me, there will be another murder in Maitland."

Josh burst out laughing. "I believe she'd do it, too."

"I guess asking you if you find anything promising to give me a call, is a waste of breath. Of course, you will. Josh, I guess we'd better get out of Becca's office and do what we do best...investigate."

They walked outside, but this time took the squad car. Madison got into the passenger's side without any arguing about who was going to drive. Josh got in, and the two just sat quietly for a moment. She turned to him, "I found a pot of gold, didn't I?"

"I had no idea when you hired her; she had that much initiative. I have to say, that I'm more than impressed."

"Me too. I have complete confidence in her. I don't feel that I have to oversee everything she's doing. She definitely has a knack for this."

"Are we finally ready to head back to Zoe's apartment?"

Madison laughed. "I suppose so unless Becca calls and *sends* us somewhere else."

Chapter Eleven

The day was quickly getting away from Madison's intended plans, but she was ready to have another look at Zoe's apartment, and this time the forensic team would be there.

She called the roommate, but he was at his girlfriend's place. He agreed to come over and let them in. When Madison and Josh drove up the team was in place and ready to begin to sweep the inside. Jon Smith was waiting outside for them. He unlocked the door but stayed outside.

The team entered first and went directly to Zoe's room. They had their latex gloves and protective coverings over their shoes and clothing. They searched the floor for any trace evidence of blood but found none. There was a strong odor of bleach in the room. Josh stepped outside to talk to the roommate.

"Jon, have you been in that room since we were here last?"

"Yes, sir."

"Can you tell me what you were doing in there?"

"Well, I figured Zoe' wasn't coming back, so I put another ad in the paper to rent the room. But when I went in there last week, it had a foul smell. My girlfriend said no one would rent that room smelling so bad, so we cleaned it."

"What did you clean it with?"

"Bleach. Why? I know it smells strong, but Ginny said if I sprayed the room with a deodorizer it would only mask the smell for a short time."

Josh turned and headed back into the room. One of the team was about to spray an area with luminol. It is used to detect the presence of blood. Blood will light up when it reacts with an oxidizing agent such as luminol. However, it will also react with other oxidizing agents such as sodium hypochlorite (bleach), certain metals, and paint.

Josh stepped into the room and reported to the forensic team that the room had been cleaned with bleach. However, they sprayed the floor looking for drag marks, and the walls for minute traces of blood. The blood on the walls can indicate the directionality of blood, giving the team a more precise spot where the crime took place.

Madison and Josh stood back as the team meticulously sprayed the entire room. Then they turned off the lights.

Madison took a long deep breath. Josh jerked backed his head and stared. There were no signs of blood on the floor nor the walls. Josh shook his head. He was sure this was the crime scene. The forensic team took photos and then left.

Madison lowered her head and walked out of the room. "I was sure we'd find something here."

"Yeah, me too."

As they left, Jon Smith approached Josh. "Detective, can I rent the room out now?"

"Huh? Oh, yes."

"Thank you."

Madison and Josh got into the squad car and just sat in silence for a moment. She turned to Josh. "I feel like we just hit a brick wall at seventy miles an hour."

"Okay, if this isn't the crime scene, then where in the hell was she murdered and by whom? Let's get some coffee."

Madison just nodded her head and then stared out of the window.

"Why don't you give your pals at the Bureau a call and see if there is anything on the soil samples?"

Madison pulled her cell phone out of her bag and called her friend, Martin.

"Hey, Madison. How's your case going?"

"Not too good right now. I was hoping you'd have something for me on the soil samples I sent you."

There was a long hesitation. "Madison, I wish I had good news for you, but unfortunately, the soil is a commonly packaged soil sold at Lowe's. It came from a large shipment from the same source and sent to several chains along the east coast. The kitty litter was also a common brand. The lab could not find any trace or specific chemical that was out of the ordinary from the manufacturer. Whoever put the dirt and litter in the back of the vehicle could have purchased it anywhere from Virginia to Key West and as far west as Texas. I'm sorry we couldn't help with that. Do you have any other leads?"

"Not yet. Either this unsub is very clever or just plain lucky, but he or she had to make a mistake somewhere and I'll find it. Thanks, Martin. Give my best to Stratton."

"Will do. Oh, are you ready to come back yet? You're missed around here."

"Not yet, but thanks," she replied and then hung up.

"Well, I take it they didn't find anything?"

Madison slammed her fist on the dashboard. "Josh, the lucky bastard used common bagged dirt and kitty litter, but he's going to make a mistake somewhere. We have to find it."

Josh kept his hands tightly on the steering wheel. "We will. Now let's get some coffee."

"I could use an extra large black coffee. This unsub is pissing me off." She tilted her head back and closed her eyes. "I need to call my sister when we get back to the office."

"Are you planning to see her?"

"No. I just want to fill her in on what has happened so she can start the background for her story. I'm sure she's going to want and to do a featured article on this when we're done, especially since the nature of this crime has already hit the news. So far, the only thing the media has is that a body was found, and I can fill her in with as much detail as we're allowed to leak at this time. She'll do Zoe justice."

That might take her mind off of our brick wall for a little while. "I'm sure she will."

They pulled into the front of the office, and Josh slapped his forehead. "I'd better go back and get Becca a coffee, or I'll have to face her wrath." *That way she'll have some privacy when she talks to her sister.*

"Okay, I'll see you shortly."

She opened the front door to see Becca on the phone. She motioned to her that she'd be in the back room, and then Becca whispered, "Just a minute."

Madison waited until Becca got off the phone. Becca looked up at Madison, "Boss, tips have been coming in all morning, but one stands out, that I think you might find interesting. Is Detective Logan coming in?"

"He'll be back shortly. What's it about?"

"Well, I've been on the phone, back and forth with Betty, comparing notes, and one tip caught our attention. It was from a taxi driver. He called Betty first and then she called me and gave me the information. I just posted on the board in the back as a possible lead. I was getting ready to call you and Detective Logan. Oh, how did it go at the apartment?"

Madison shook her head. "We found nothing there today, but I have that nagging gut feeling that something did happen there. I'm beginning to think that might be the reason someone got rid of our victim's belongings. I need to call Denise McClain and ask her if she can identify any of the items we found in the maintenance man's place."

I thought you already did that?"

"I put it off to give her time to grieve, but she might be able to shed some light on this case, so I plan to talk to her again. Now, what did you and Betty uncover today?"

Becca got up from her desk and started down the hall, just as Josh came in the front door. "Anyone need a coffee?" he hollered.

Becca turned to Madison and whispered. "Did you have him do that?"

"No, he thought of it on his own."

Becca took the coffee and led them to the case room.

Josh tugged at his ear and looked at Madison. Madison just shrugged her shoulders and smiled. "Becca has a lead."

He turned with his eyes wide open, raising his eyebrows. "*She* has a lead?"

They walked into the case room, and Madison took a seat and then motioned for Josh to do the same.

She pulled her shoulders back, stepped to the board and started to qualify the leads. "As you can see we, Betty and me, have been categorizing the leads coming in from the TV spot. I've labeled them as possible prank calls, low priority, high priority. As you have made it very clear, we don't rule out anyone until all the facts are in." she said nodding to Madison. "But the one that came in this morning while you were at Zoe's, I believe has the most promise. Betty got the call and forwarded it to *us*. It was from a taxi driver. He stated that the same night that Ms. McClain's car was left in the parking lot, he picked up a man at the airport."

Josh interrupted. "What made him think that had some connection?"

Becca sighed and took a deep breath. "Because the man had no luggage. He said he was from out of town visiting a friend, and he asked to let off only a mile from Ms.McClain's apartment."

Josh crinkled his nose. "I see this as a coincidence, but we'll talk to him."

"That's not all. He wanted to pay with a local coupon, but if he were from out of town why did he have the coupon?"

Madison leaned over the table looking at the board. "Did the driver get a look at the guy?"

"No, he didn't. It was too dark. He said he was tired and wasn't paying that much attention. He thinks he was about 5'10, and medium build, but couldn't tell anything else. He said he thought the guy had a beard but wasn't sure. However, the passenger did give a name, Frank Butler."

Madison jumped up, grabbed Josh's arm. "Let's talk to this Frank Butler."

Before she could get out of the door, Becca hollered out. "We couldn't find records on any of the flights that night with that name."

Josh stopped in the hall and blew out a puff of air. "Does the driver remember exactly where he dropped off this so-called passenger?"

Becca handed him a piece of paper with the address. He turned to Madison. "You ready to pound the streets?"

She ran her fingers through her hair. "What else do we have to do right now? Becca, good work."

"Sorry, I couldn't give you better information."

"No, that's okay. You gave us a lead; now we need to see if we can find this person and ask him some questions. Thank you. You're doing a great job."

Josh was already half-way out the door before Madison caught up with him. Josh opened the driver's side of the squad car, but stood there with his hand on the roof of the car as Madison walked around to the other side."It's been a while since I've had to pound the pavement looking for someone. I hope it won't lead to a dead end."

"Me too. So far, our leads are going nowhere. Let's talk to this taxi driver first."

"Okay."

They called the cab company and it just so happened the driver from that night was in the area and agreed to meet with them in front of the Police station. He had just dropped off a fare and had nowhere to go until his next pickup.

Josh escorted the taxi driver to the front seat of the squad car. Madison sat in the back as they interviewed him. Josh wanted to hear first hand of the accounts of that evening. "Can you give me as much detail as you can about that night?"

"Well, I got a call to pick up a Frank Butler, who was coming in from a flight, so I waited out in front of the terminal at the Sanford Orlando International Airport."

"What time was that?"

The taxi driver opened his Ipod. "It was 10:21 p.m."

"Okay, continue."

"I had stopped first to get a cup of coffee at that Quick Stop before driving in. I sat in front of the terminal drinking my coffee, and then my passenger got into the back seat. I looked in the rear-view mirror, but all I could see was a dark figure with a hoody pulled over his head. When I asked his name, he said Frank Butler. I asked him if he wanted me to get his luggage, but all he said was he had none. I thought that was a bit strange. I pick up a lot of strange characters, so that didn't stick in my mind at first."

Madison leaned forward from the back seat. "Where did he want you to take him?"

"He just handed me a piece of paper with an address."

"Do you still have that paper?"

"Nope. If I kept every piece of paper people gave me, I'd have to have a file. I just set my GPS and tossed the note in my trash and headed for the address. Then it started getting strange."

Josh leaned back with his arm over the back of his seat. "In what way was it strange?"

"The address he gave me was an empty lot. When we got there, I mentioned that I must have entered the address wrong, but he said that would be fine, and then he handed me a coupon for a portion of the fare. I asked him about the coupon because they are only for locals, and he said he was from out of town. His answer was that a friend sent it to him. It didn't add up and to tell you the truth I was eager to get this guy out of my cab, so I took the coupon anyway. He started creeping me out."

"Did you see what direction he was headed when he got out of your cab?"

"I didn't think I did because I just wanted to get out of there and pick up another ride, but the more I thought about it I remembered him heading for a neighborhood down the street."

"Can you give us a description of the person?"

"Not really. It was dark where I let him out, and his clothes were big and baggy and he was hunched over most of the time while he was walking. It was hard to tell if he was tall or not by the way he walked, but he couldn't have been too built or his clothes would have fit better. Sorry, I can't be of more help."

"You were a great deal of help. Thank you." Josh handed him his card. "If you can think of anything else, give me a call."

"I sure will. If this is all you need from me right now, I've got a pickup to make."

"That's fine."

The taxi driver drove off, and Madison hopped back up in the front seat. "Well, not too much to go on, but we can start knocking on doors."

Josh adjusted himself and snapped on his seatbelt. He turned and smiled at her. "Looks like we'll be doing some old fashion detective work. I haven't had to knock on doors in a long time. I hope you're wearing your walking shoes. We have a few houses to visit."

They drove into the area the taxi driver said he dropped off his passenger. Madison took one side of the street and Josh the other. They knocked on every door hoping someone saw something that night. Her hopes were sinking with each house. Most of the people they talked to were either too old, families with children who didn't see or hear anything. Madison glanced across the street, but all Josh did was shrug his shoulders. They had visited every house on that block with nothing to show for it.

It was getting late, and they both were feeling the stress of the day and the lack of leads. The case threatened to come to a stand still.

Madison slumped across the dashboard. "I'm drawing a blank, and I'm exhausted. You feel like calling it a day?"

Josh turned toward her. "Maybe tomorrow we can review the board and see what we have and where to go from here. I'll drop you off at the office."

She said very little on the drive back. Her feet were throbbing, her back hurt and her ego felt trampled on. *What in the hell am I not seeing? It's always something I'm overlooking, something staring me in the face, and I can't see it. I hate this.* "Yeah, that's a good idea. I'm drawing a blank right now. I'll see you in the morning."

When Josh dropped her off, she went inside expecting to see Becca. She glanced at the ornate clock in the reception area. "Crap, we went non-stop all day and got nowhere. No wonder she went home. Maybe I should do the same." But she had to go to the board one more time. She stood there staring at it as though it would miraculously show her who the killer was. She

140 The Dark Side of Secrets

wanted to erase the entire board and start over, but left the room and slammed the door behind her.

She got in her car and drove home. Sophie was waiting at the door spinning in circles and wagging her tail. "You have no idea what a crazy day I've had." Sophie jumped up on her leg to be petted, and then turned and raced to the back doors. Madison dropped her bag and files on the counter, kicked off her shoes and sauntered to the French doors and opened them. Sophie immediately raced to the backyard, sniffing the ground, looking for that perfect spot. Madison headed for her bedroom. She dropped her clothes in a pile on the chair and slipped into her yoga pants and over-sized Gator sweatshirt. Her frustration with the case was eating at her. She poured herself a glass of wine and walked out on the patio and sat at the little Bistro table while Sophie roamed through the yard.

She heard Becca's sliding glass doors open next door. Becca was carrying her glass of wine. Sophie gave a *hello* yelp and Becca turned toward Madison's yard. Madison called out, "Want to join me for a glass of wine?"

"Sure."

Becca walked out her back gate over to Madison's. She opened the gate, and Sophie was spinning in circles when she saw her. "Well, hello girl." She bent down and stroked Sophie and then joined Madison at the table.

"What a day," Becca said, sipping her wine.

"I know, and yet still we can't catch a break. This case has me stumped. I feel like we're missing the obvious. I just left the office after staring at our leads and timeline. I can't see a pattern yet."

"I know what you mean. I was tempted to erase the entire board and start over, but I was afraid it would throw you off."

Madison chuckled. "I felt the same way. I just wanted to clear the board and start the case from the beginning."

"Becca set her wine glass on the table. "Madison, I might be overstepping here, but that might not be a bad idea. I've seen how you operate. You haven't even formulated a profile of your killer yet. What if, just a thought, I erase the board tomorrow and you and Josh approach this case as if you were just given a homicide case. We've been working the missing person's angle. However, that has been solved, and we now have a new case."

"Damn, Becca, that's brilliant. Why didn't I see that? We have been trying to melt the two cases together. Zoe McClain has been located…case closed. Now we have a new case… a murder victim, and an unknown killer. I need to look at the facts again, formulate a profile and work it from there." She slapped the top of the table and grinned. "Are you ready for another glass of wine?"

Becca laughed, "I am."

Chapter Twelve

Madison woke up early that morning feeling refreshed and excited about starting their *new* case. Though it was just an extension of the one she was working on, it gave her a renewed direction and focus. She showered, dressed and sat in the living room drinking her morning coffee as Sophie was outside with her morning ritual. She was eager to share with Josh what she and Becca talked about last night but didn't want to disturb him so early. She turned up her coffee cup for that last sip and started for the kitchen for another cup when her cell phone rang. It was Josh. *What is he doing up this early?*

"Hart," she answered.

"Detective Logan, here at this end," he joked.

"What are you doing up this early?"

"I couldn't sleep last night. I kept thinking about our case, and I wanted to run something past you before you headed to the office."

"Okay, why don't you swing by my place? I just made a fresh pot of coffee."

Before she could say another word he blurted out, "I'm on my way." He hung up just as she was about to ask him to pick up some donuts. She was feeling good and wanted something other than the usual bagels. She poured out the remaining coffee and made a fresh pot.

Within minutes, there was a knock on the door. Sophie darted from the back yard and raced past Madison to the front door. Sophie sniffed the threshold and gave out one yelp. Madison teased her. "Who do you think it is, girl?" Sophie spun in circles and tried to squeeze her nose as close to the door as possible, so when the door opened, she could be the first to greet Josh. Madison slowly opened the door and watched as Sophie squeezed her nose out. "Good morning, girl," Josh smiled.

Josh was standing at the door with a dozen of Krispy Kreme donuts. "I can't believe you brought donuts, but a dozen?" she snickered. "Were you planning a party?"

"No. They had a sale this morning, and I expected it was going to be a kick-ass day and we could all use a sugar jolt."

"You did, did you? And what brought you to that conclusion, since we were at a stand-still when I left you last night?"

Josh walked around the counter to the cabinet, pulled out a mug and poured himself some coffee, grabbed a powdered donut and headed for the couch.

"Make yourself at home, why don't you." She smiled.

"Oh, I'm sorry. Did you want another cup?"

She just shook her head, topped off her cup with hot coffee and joined him. She curled up in the overstuffed chair across from him watching as he attacked the donut and sipped his coffee. "You seem to be in a good mood this morning. Did I miss something after you left?"

"Not exactly." He set his cup down and finished his donut. Madison bit her lower lip to keep from laughing. *I don't know why he buys those powdered donuts. He wears most it on his shirt.* "Do you need a napkin?"

"Huh?"

She pointed to his chest. "Your shirt."

He glanced down at the white sugar dust all over the front of him. "I thought you were going to remind me not to buy that kind," he said as he brushed the powder off into his hand.

"You'd think you'd remember without me bringing it to your attention," she laughed.

He got up and went into the hall bathroom to make sure he got it all, then freshened his coffee, and sat down again.

"There, are you finished pointing out what a mess I am?"

She just smiled and shook her head. "Now, what are you so excited about this morning?"

"You're probably going to think I'm crazy, but the more I agonized over this case last night, the more I wondered if our approach is all wrong."

She took another sip of her coffee. "What do you mean?"

"Okay, I'm going to start from the top, so listen to what I have to say before you throw it out. You were hired to find a missing woman, right?"

"Yes."

"Well, you did that. That case is closed. Now we have a new case, a homicide. Just because they are of the same person, it is a new case. Why don't we start over? I mean from scratch. Let's begin our investigation with the murder of Zoe McClain. Before you squash my theory, just give it some thought." He leaned back on the couch waiting for her response.

"Great idea."

He jerked forward. "What?"

"I said, it's a great idea."

"You mean you're not going to argue with me?"

"Nope. I'll call Becca this morning and tell her to erase the board and tell her we're going to start from the beginning of this crime."

Josh dropped his jaw for a moment, then pulled back his shoulders, tilted his head back and clenched his hands over his head. "Okay then."

Madison was not about to burst his bubble and tell him she and Becca had already decided that on their own, but it was amazing to her that he came up with it at the same time.

They finished their coffee and Josh managed to down another donut, but this time he opted for a cake one without any coating. He grabbed the box and headed out the door. "I'll see you in a few minutes. I've got to run by McDonalds and get a coffee for Becca. Do want another cup, too?"

"Yes, I think I'm going to need a lot of caffeine today."

As soon as he closed the door, she called Becca. "Hey Becca, when Josh tells you of his great idea, try and sound surprised and enthused. He thought of the same thing we did, but I don't want him to think it wasn't his idea, at least for now."

"I get it. No problem. I won't erase the board until you come in and discuss it all over again."

"Thanks. I'll be in shortly."

Madison wanted to let Josh arrive first. She knew he would tell Becca the moment he got there to see her reaction. He was so proud of himself for coming up with the idea. She laid down a few potty pads on the bathroom floor for Sophie in case it was going to be a long day. She put a fresh bowl of water and some dried dog food down too, although Sophie never ate her food until Madison returned home.

I guess he's there by now. She grabbed her bag and stack of papers and headed for the front door. "See you later. You be a good girl." Sophie ran to the overstuffed chair, jumped up and laid her head on the armrest.

Madison drove slowly down the street to give Josh time to explain his theory to Becca. She opened the door, but they were already in the back waiting for her. The box of donuts sat opened on the table. Someone had already eaten several, and she knew it wasn't Becca. With Josh's nervous energy, he ate more than usual. *I'll bet he's not even aware how many he's had. He is going to be on such a sugar rush for a while and then take a nose dive later. I'd better close this box before he devoured them all.*

"I see you have told Becca of your idea. What do you think, Becca?"

"He has a point. Do you want me to clear the board?"

"Yes, we might as well start over and see what we can come up with."

Josh sat down and started to open the donut box when Madison pretended not to notice and grabbed the box. "I'll clear off the table so we can sort through the evidence."

Josh furrowed his brow. "Uh, what are you going to do with that box?"

"Oh, I'm sorry. I thought you were finished. You must have eaten six. You want to save the rest for later?"

"I didn't have that many. I only had two."

She cocked her head, raised her eyebrow, twitched her lips and slowly opened the box.

"I didn't eat all those," he grumbled.

He looked up at Becca. "Didn't you have some?"

"Not yet."

"Well, crap," he moaned. "Put that box out of my sight."

Madison set the box behind her and began laying out the papers and bagged evidence.

"Here's what I'd like to do first. Let's list our persons of interest across the top and below each name write as much as we know about them. Then see if any of them had means, motive or opportunity. Becca, this time I'd like to add the roommate's girlfriend to that list. If we're going to start from the beginning, I want to know where each person was at the time Zoe's car was parked at the airport. Then, Josh, you and I can re-interview the neighbors. Also, I'd like to go over the car again to see if we missed anything the first time."

"Becca while we're gone, would you mind organizing the boards? Let's use the other board, for now, to outline what we know about our victim and the pieces of evidence we have and see if we can find a link."

"I'm on it, Boss."

Madison felt a rush of adrenaline race through her body. This is the way she was accustomed to dealing with a crime. Once the pieces of Zoe's death were in place, she could present a profile, and update Chief Baker on something with promise.

She and Josh headed outside. Josh started for the squad car, but Madison was already opening the driver's side of her car. Josh raced around the car and jumped into the passenger's side. There was no trying to talk her into them taking the squad car. His Maddy had a hold of a bone and wasn't going to let go. Her steam and direction was back, and he was sure it was all because of his new idea. He loved watching her in action when she was on a roll. Nothing was going to get her way.

She slammed on her brakes in front of Zoe's apartment, just as Jon Smith was leaving. "Mr. Smith, do you have a moment?"

"Well, I was on my way to work. Can it wait?"

"Not really. We'd like to get back into the apartment and look at Zoe's room again."

He gave a heavy sigh and turned around to let them in. The entire time Madison and Josh were looking over the apartment, he kept looking down at his watch and fidgeting. "I hate to rush you, but I don't want to be late for work."

"We're almost done here, for now," Josh chimed in.

"For now? What more do you expect to find? The room is empty; your people have sprayed the entire place, and I need to rent it out as soon as possible."

They continued until they finished what they needed to do. "Thank you," Madison mumbled as she passed him on her way out. Josh just nodded. Mr. Smith followed them out and immediately raced to his car and sped out of the complex.

Josh watched as Smith took off. "I sure hope he's not late." Josh turned to her. "Where to now? Are we going to interview the neighbors?"

"No, not yet. I want to talk to Doc Webb again and then check out the car."

Josh leaned over the dashboard.

"Josh, are you okay?"

"Yeah, but my gut hurts. I hope I'm not coming down with something."

Madison quickly turned away and bit her lip. She composed herself and turned to him. "You don't suppose a half a dozen donuts have anything to do with your gut hurting, do you?"

"Don't be a smart-ass. I didn't have that many." He buckled over for a moment and then he tried to sit up straight. "Let's just go." She pulled out of the parking spot and headed toward the cul-de-sac at the end of the street to turn around. As they passed one of the houses, Madison noticed a figure standing at the window watching them. "Did you see someone in that window?"

"You mean the old lady that's peering out of her curtains? Yes, I saw her. That's someone we haven't interviewed yet. We'll put her down as someone to come back to."

"I don't imagine much gets past her on this street."

"That's what I was thinking." He smiled.

She wanted to get his mind off of his cramping stomach. "That's what makes us such a good team," she smiled.

The big grin that came across his face said it all.

As they drove to the lab, Madison heard Josh's occasional groan. She felt sorry for him. He was suffering. *I'll bet he won't be too eager to finish off the rest of those donuts anytime soon.* They parked at the back of the lab. Madison headed to see Doc, but Josh disappeared the moment they entered the building. Doc was sitting at his desk with his reading glasses resting on the tip of his nose. When he saw her come in, he stood to greet her. "Ms. Hart. What brings you to see me?" He straightened his bow tie and ran his fingers through his tousled hair. "Please forgive my appearance. I've been shuffling papers and finishing up my report on your young woman."

"That's why I'm here. What can you tell me about the way you found her?"

"What do you mean?"

"I'm trying to pull together a profile on her killer. The way the body was positioned can tell me a lot about our unsub."

Doc scratched his head and squinted his eyes. "I'm not sure what you're looking for."

"Just describe the process of uncovering her body. If you could go through what you've done, step by step; how she was covered and in what manner the body appeared to be."

"I see what you're hoping to find. Okay. After we removed the dirt…"

She interrupted him. "Did the dirt and litter look like it was all just dumped on her suddenly or meticulously placed?"

"It was evenly distributed which leads me to believe it was carefully placed on her. As I was saying; after we removed the dirt, we discovered she had been covered with a blanket, and under that, a sheet covered her body and head. Though her body took some maneuvering to fit in the trunk of that compact car, it was placed in a normal fetal position, almost as if she were sleeping."

"Thank you, Doc."

"Did that give you what you needed?"

"It did."

Josh entered the room looking a little pale. "Are you alright, Detective?" Doc asked.

"Yes, I just ate something that didn't agree with me, but I feel okay now."

Madison rolled her eyes. *I'd say.* "Feeling better?"

"Yep. Now what did you learn," he replied quickly changing the subject.

"I think I'm formulating a profile of our unsub, but I need a little more. Doc, is the car still in the garage?"

"It is. I think Joey is down there doing another finer sift through the dirt looking for any minute particles we may have missed in our first look."

"Thank you, Doc."

They headed around to the back garage. Joey was sifting the dirt and placing random samples into his Maspectrometer to see if he could identify any other chemicals present.

Josh stepped up behind Joey. "I thought you were a coroner?"

"I am, but my passion is in forensic pathology. When we're slow in the lab, Doc lets me work on projects here. I was hoping to discover some foreign particles that don't belong in these dirt samples. How can I help you?"

Madison walked over to Zoe's car. "I wanted to sit in her car."

Joey pulled on his earlobe. "You just want to sit there?"

Josh tapped him on the shoulder. "Don't ask."

Madison got into the driver's side and just sat there. She held onto the steering wheel, opened the glove compartment and reached under the seat, and then sat back against the seat. Josh remained quiet and stood back. He wasn't sure what she was doing. By the way Madison was immersing herself into the comfort of the car, he suspected she was putting herself in the mind of the driver. She turned the car on, and reached over and tapped the button on the radio. Suddenly, the blast of hard rock blared throughout the lab. She pushed the button to off, and sat back again and was still.

Josh approached the car. "Anything you want to share?"

"Not yet, but this is telling me more about who drove this car last."

Joey came up behind Josh and whispered. "Does she do that often?"

Josh stood with his jacket opened and his hands on his hips. "Only when she's following a clue."

"Huh?"

Josh whispered, "She's onto something, and if I were you, I'd remain very quiet until she's finished."

Joey cautiously backed up and leaned against the table as he watched her.

Madison reached down and grabbed the handle to adjust the seat. She pulled on it, but it won't move. She jerked harder. It seemed to be hung up on something. She got out of the car, bent down and looked under the front seat. "Josh, would you bring me a flashlight?"

Joey pointed to one by the sink but said nothing. Josh just carried it to her, placed it in her hand while she continued looking under the seat. Pointing the light directly toward the area just on the other side of where the seat slides, she saw an object. "Josh, pass me a glove."

Josh handed her a latex glove. She slid it on her left hand and reached under the seat. She tugged and twisted until whatever was there broke loose. She lay back on the floorboard shining a light on the object. "Josh, I need my cell phone and an evidence bag."

He handed her the cell phone and pulled a baggie out of his pocket and gave it to her. "Did you find something?"

"Yeah."

She snapped a picture and then sealed the object and handed it to Josh and then slid out of the car. Josh held up the bag to the light. "Looks like a watch."

"I think it got caught while someone adjusted the seat, and it lodged. That's why the seat wouldn't move forward. I suspect it happened after Zoe's death. There is no way she could have driven this car with the seat in that position."

Josh stared at the watch. "Is that a hair stuck in this band?"

Madison took the bag and held it to the light. There was a small strand of black hair attached to the band of the watch. "Let's get this over to the lab." She started out the back door without saying a word to Joey.

Joey followed Josh to the door. "That partner of yours is a strange one."

Josh just grinned.

They left the coroner's and immediately drove over to the lab. Madison wanted to find out if that was Zoe's hair or possibly that of their unsub. Either way, she was fairly sure it had been lodged under the seat after Zoe's body was placed in the trunk. "What can you tell me, Bob?"

Bob laid the hair on the sterile stainless steel table and took a pair of forceps and plucked the hair from the band. He placed it under a high-powered microscope. He adjusted the lens and turned the strand of hair several times. "Well, we have enough to determine it is human hair, but other than that, I'll have to take DNA from it to find out if it's a man or a woman."

Josh leaned over the table and shot a picture of the watch and hair. "How soon can you get to this. It involves an ongoing murder investigation."

"Yeah, and so are all those trays on the shelf over there, but I should be able to take a sample and send it off later this afternoon, but can't promise how soon we'll get the results."

Madison smiled and in her soft-spoken voice she said, "Thank you, Bob. I appreciate your help."

"For you, Ms. Hart, I'll put a rush on it."

Josh grit his teeth and shook his head. *For you, Ms. Hart, I'll put a rush on it. What a chump. I could have given him a twenty dollar bill and he'd still put it on the shelf.*

They walked back out to the car. Josh was still shaking his head when he sat down. "What that about?" she asked.

"What's what about?"

"You're shaking your head, and that look on your face."

"Ah, nothing. I just can't believe how some men can melt when a sweet talking woman asks them to do something. The guy was putty in your hands. I could have slipped a twenty and still got nothing."

She looked at him and waggled her eyebrow. "I know, it's shocking, isn't it?"

"Well, you got the job done."

"Looks like we have a good start to our case. Why don't we stop by Patsio's and grab a couple of sandwiches before we head back to see how Becca is doing with the board?

Josh smiled. "I was wondering if you were going to stop and eat."

They pulled into the parking lot at Patsio's, a small Greek diner. The place had been there for nearly forty years. The old cook was now the owner but still did the cooking. The moment he saw Madison walk in, he hollered out from behind the pass-through from the kitchen. "Is that Maddy Hart?"

She turned to see him darting out of the kitchen. He opened his arms and embraced her. "Look at you. I haven't seen you in years. Are you living back here now?"

She gasped for breath after the hug. "I am. It's great to see you too. Mom always said you cooked the best Greek food around."

"Sorry to hear about your Mom. What are you doing now, I heard you went to work for the Feds?"

"Marty, this is Detective Logan."

"I know Josh. He comes in here a lot. Now, what about you? What are you up to these days? Is the FBI working on a case here?"

She smiled. "Well, no. I've opened up a Private Investigation Agency in Maitland, and right now I'm assisting Detective Logan on a case."

He slapped his hand over his mouth. "You're not working on that case where they found that young girl's body in the trunk of a car, are you?"

Josh interjected. "As a matter of fact we are."

Marty lowered his head. "That's just terrible. I sure hope you find who did that." He looked back at Madison and smiled. "What can I fix for you today?"

"I'd like two of those Gyros."

"I'll have one of those too, Marty," Josh added.

Marty smiled. "You must really like my Gyros, Miss Maddy."

She grinned. "I do." She didn't tell him that one of them was for Becca.

Josh hollered out to Marty, "Can we have those to go?"

"Sure thing, Josh."

They sat at the counter and watched Marty through the pass-through as he whipped together his famous sandwiches. He returned with them boxed up, and when Josh tried to pay, Marty put his hand over Josh's hand. "Your money is no good in here today. Enjoy!"

Madison reached over and hugged Marty. "Thank you. It's so good to see you again."

"Maddy, don't be a stranger."

"I won't."

Madison got into the car and just sat for a moment. Josh was eager to get back to the office and eat. "Are you okay, Maddy?"

"Yes. Seeing Marty again brought back memories of Mom and me coming in on Sunday mornings to share his Eggs Benedict. I miss Mom."

Josh reached over and patted her on the shoulder. She smiled and then started up the car. "We've got a case to solve."

Chapter Thirteen

By the time Madison and Josh returned to the office, Becca had completely reorganized the board. She had all the people of interest written across the top with the information they had gathered on each one written beneath their names. On the other board was Zoe's name and her timeline of the last week of her life.

On the unsub board, she wrote the names according to the last time they said they had any contact with Zoe. Jon Smith was the last known person to see her, but he had an air-tight alibi. His girlfriend stated he was with her the entire weekend, which gives an alibi for each of them unless they were in it together. Madison didn't feel that was the case based on the way the body was put in the trunk. And apparently her close friend and ex-boyfriend was the last person to hear from her. He claims Zoe wanted to talk to him about something that she was concerned about, but he supposedly never got back with her. Then they have the guy who was stalking her, the cable installer, and the maintenance man.

Madison stood in front of the boards glancing back and forth between the two. "It seems we have quite a line-up of characters, and I'm not ruling out any of them just yet. Based on the condition of the body when it was found, I'd say whoever put her in there felt some remorse. He, or she, carefully laid the body and took the time to cover her well with the sheet and blanket before loading the dirt on top of her. Our unsub didn't want to disturb her. I don't think the intention was to murder our victim. I think something got out of hand and escalated, causing our perp to kill her."

Josh pulled back his jacket, put his hands on his hips and stepped up next to Madison. "Yeah, but if her murder took place in her room then why was there no blood evidence? We know she was shot."

"That's the puzzle. Either she was lured someplace else and killed, or someone tossed the evidence with her things. We don't have all her belongings. I want to talk to Zoe's mom again and go over the items we've located and see if she can piece together Zoe's room and tell us what we're missing."

Becca chimed in. "I know you believe whoever did this felt some remorse, but if it was a spur of the moment thing, then don't you think we would have found some blood evidence. This is shaping up to look more like premeditated murder to me…unless we haven't found a critical piece of evidence yet."

Madison and Josh turned to Becca. Madison tilted her head and grinned. "You're right! I'm going to visit Denise McClain this afternoon. Josh, do you want to check with the old lady who was watching us leave the complex and see if she saw anything?"

"Okay. I'll call you later." Josh grabbed his sandwich and headed for the front door. Madison asked Becca if she would get all of the photos of the items found. Becca had the photos in a separate file and just handed the entire file to Madison. "What would I do without you, Becca. Thanks. Call me if you hear anything from the lab."

"I sure will, Boss."

Madison started out the door.

"Boss, aren't you going to eat first?"

"Would you mind putting my sandwich in the fridge. I need to follow up on this. I'll eat it later."

Becca watched as Madison left. *She hasn't eaten anything today. I hope she doesn't overdo and run herself down again.* Becca wrapped up the Gyro and put it in the fridge. She knew Madison wasn't going to eat it, but she did as her boss asked.

Madison dreaded having to drag Denise through all the emotional heartache again, but it was crucial to finding her daughter's killer. She would know her daughter's room better than anyone else.

Denise was standing outside waiting for Madison. "Good morning Ms. Hart. I'm so glad you came. I didn't have a chance to properly thank you for all you did to find Zoe."

Madison reached for Denise's hand. "You're welcome. I just wish things could have turned out for the good. I'm so sorry."

"At least I was able to bring her home and give her a proper burial and for that I am thankful. How can I help you today? Oh, I'm sorry, please, come inside," she softly spoke, motioning Madison inside the house. "Can I get you a cup of tea?"

"No, thank you. I have a few photos of various items we've recovered. Are you sure you're up to this?"

"Certainly, I want to help in any way I can to find out who did this to my daughter."

Madison took the pictures out of her bag and laid them on the dining room table. She hesitated for a moment when she heard Denise sniffle. "Are you sure about this?"

"Yes."

Madison continued placing the pictures down, and one by one, Denise picked them up. Then she laid them all back down on the table, got up and left the room. Madison knew this was going to be difficult for Denise, but it had to be done. She sat back in her chair and waited. Moments later Denise entered the room with tears streaming down her cheeks. She was carrying a framed picture of Zoe. She placed it down in front of Madison. "You can take this with you until you catch who did this."

Madison picked it up. It was a picture of Zoe smiling.

Denise leaned over and pointed. "This was taken shortly after Zoe moved into her new apartment. She was so proud of how she had modestly decorated it. I snapped this from the doorway. It shows almost everything that was in her room." Then she handed Madison a few more photos taken from different angles showing every item in the room. It was exactly what Madison needed. She wouldn't have to burden Denise with showing her all the items that they found. She wanted Denise to remember Zoe in that room and how happy she was, not discarded items discovered in the trash or someone else's home.

"Thank you. These photos will be very helpful. I'll make sure you get these back as soon as we close the case."

Denise walked Madison to the door and hugged her. "If there is anything else I can do to help, please let me do it for Zoe."

Madison patted her on the shoulder. "I will."

Josh pulled up in front of the home of the lady who had watched him and Madison drive away from the apartment complex earlier. She was sitting in a chair by the window pretending to be reading. Josh suspected not much got past this woman. He rang the doorbell and waited. After a few moments, he rang it again. Just as he was about to ring it for the third time, an elderly woman opened the door but left the screen door locked. "Yes?" she asked.

Josh pulled out his badge. "I'm Detective Logan of the Maitland Police Department, and we're investigating the death of one of your neighbors. I was wondering if you had a moment?" He pulled out a photo of Zoe and showed it to the woman.

"For what?" She snapped.

"I'd like to ask you some questions about some of your neighbors."

"Okay, but you better not try and pull any funny stuff. I have a gun."

"Oh no, ma'am. This is strictly related to our investigation."

She unlocked the screen door and motioned for him to enter. "You can sit in that chair over there," she said pointing to a chair across the coffee table from where she was sitting.

Josh stood until she took her seat and then sat in his appointed chair. She smiled seeing him stand until she sat. "You seem like a nice young man. Would you like a cup of coffee?"

"No, thank you. I just finished a cup." He hesitated for a moment then began to ask her a few questions. "As I mentioned, the Police Department is investigating the murder of one of your neighbors, Zoe McClain. She lived in the apartment across the cul-de-sac from here.

She went missing a couple of weeks ago on a weekend. Did you see anything out of the ordinary that weekend or any unusual vehicles coming and going?"

"I don't sleep well, so I like to sit here and read in the evenings. I didn't notice anything odd that weekend, but," she hesitated.

Josh was going to have to pry it out of her. "Did you see or hear anything before then?"

"Well, I did see the young woman you're asking about one evening in the parking lot before she disappeared."

Josh hesitated, thinking she would add more to her statement. He took a deep breath. "What was she doing?"

"She was arguing with someone."

"Do you remember what night that was, and approximately what time?"

"Of course, I do. I'm not senile."

"No ma'am."

"It was Wednesday night about 11:00 p.m."

Josh bit his lip waiting for more information.

"Young man, would you like a cup of coffee?"

"No, thank you, I just finished a cup."

"What is it you wanted to know?"

He leaned forward in his chair. "Can you describe the person she was arguing with?"

"Who she was arguing with?"

"Who was your neighbor, Zoe, arguing with on that Wednesday night before she went missing."

"Oh, why didn't you say so. She was arguing with a man in the parking lot. I could hear them screaming, but couldn't see him very well. His back was to me, but then he pushed her against the car. She slapped him and ran back to her apartment, and he got into his truck and sped out of the complex. All I can say is it's a good thing it wasn't during the day when the children are playing in the street, or he could have run over one of them."

"Did you get a good look at the truck?"

"What truck?"

"The truck that belonged to the man who was arguing with your neighbor?"

"Not really. It was dark, and some of those street lights are out. I've been complaining to the manager about fixing those lights, but nothing has been done about it yet."

"Could you tell if it was a pickup truck and if it was a dark or a light color?"

"What pickup truck?"

Josh leaned back in his seat and placed his hands on his head. "Could you see what kind of truck it was that the man who was arguing with Zoe drove off in? And whether the truck was a dark or light color?"

"Well, let me think about that for a moment." Josh wanted to pull his hair out but sat patiently anticipating he'd have to repeat the entire scenario over again.

"I believe it was a 1994 Dodge pickup. The top was either dark red or green. My eyes aren't what they used to be, but I know my trucks. Oh, and it had a wide silver band along the bottom of the truck."

Josh jerked his head, and his eyes widened. "That's a pretty good description. Is there anything else you can remember about that night or any other night that weekend?"

The old lady yawned. "What weekend?"

"I've taken up enough of your time, but if you can remember anything else, please give me a call." He handed her his card and walked to the door.

"Thank you for coming by and visiting," she smiled. "I hope you'll stop by again when you're in the neighborhood."

Josh smiled and nodded his head. "Yes, ma'am."

She closed the door, and he heard the lock turn. As he got into his car, he turned back toward the house. She had already resumed her position in front of the window watching the world outside. He sat in the car wondering if the information the old lady gave him was credible or was she thumbing through her past creating what she thought she saw that night. Either way, he would follow up. *I hope Maddy was able to find out more from Mrs. McClain.*

It was nearly 6:30 p.m. before Josh returned to the office. No one was there. He drove past Madison's, and her car wasn't there either, so he headed home. It was a long day, but he felt they were making progress. He wanted to shower and have a beer, before checking with Madison. *If the old lady was right, and Zoe was arguing with a man outside her apartment that night, it wouldn't hurt to check and see if any our suspects owned a truck matching her description. Ah, hell, I'm beat. It will wait until tomorrow.* He finished his beer, popped the cap off of another one and turned on the evening news. He changed out of his suit into a pair of old faded jeans and T-shirt and plopped on the couch. He wasn't paying that much attention to what was on TV. He thought about that truck. *How difficult would it be for me to cruise the area where the suspects lived and see if I can spot one that fit the description?* He took one more sip of his beer and headed out the door. He would start at the ex-boyfriend.

He pulled into McDonald's and ordered a large black coffee, hoping it would take the edge off the effects of the beer. He was halfway down 17-92 towards the home of David George when his cell phone rang. It was Madison.

"Hey, how did your day go?

It's still going. Are you busy?" she replied.

"No, I'm just driving around. Why?"

"Can you come by my place? I want to show you what Denise gave me. I think between the two of us and the photos of the items we found, we can see what might be missing. How soon can you get here?"

"I should be there in about fifteen minutes."

"Great. I'll order us pizza?"

"Sounds good. Do I need to pick up something for us to drink?"

"That won't be necessary. I felt like having a beer tonight, so I picked up a six-pack of Samuel Adams."

"Great. I'll be there shortly."

Madison quickly ran through the shower and put on her yoga pants and a hooded sweatshirt. She pulled out the pictures from Denise, along with the framed one and set them next the photos of the items found.

The doorbell rang, and Sophie ran to the door and barked. It wasn't her usual yelp when Josh was there. She peeked through the peephole. It was the pizza delivery. She opened the door, paid the man, and took the box and set it on the counter.

She barely had the box opened when the bell rang again, only this time Sophie gave a little yelp and rushed to the door and sniffed the threshold. "Who is it, Sophie?" Madison teased. Sophie began to do her spinning in circles waiting for her to open the door, and when she did, Sophie darted out the door to greet Josh. "One thing I can always count on when I come over is being greeted by a beautiful redhead."

He leaned down and petted her, then closed the door. He headed straight for the pizza. "Good, I'm starving." He put two slices on a paper plate and handed it to Madison.

"What makes you think I want two?"

"I figured if you didn't eat the other one, I would," he remarked as he put two slices on another plate. He opened the fridge and pulled out a beer. "You want one?"

"I've got mine already."

She stood watching how comfortable he was in her place and how sexy he looked in those tight jeans and T-shirt. Her eyes followed him to the couch. He took a big bite of his pizza, a swig of the beer and then set them both down. He fixed his gaze on the photos on the coffee table. "Where did these other pictures come from?"

"Denise gave them to me this afternoon. It was difficult for her to relive all this again, but I think these pictures will give us a better vision of how Zoe lived in that room and what belongs to her from these other items."

Josh picked up the framed photo. "She looks so happy in this picture. When was it taken?"

"Her mother said she took this just after Zoe finished decorating her room. She liked things simple and sparse, so she had room to work in the evenings preparing the next day's assignments for her students."

Josh picked up one of several of the items found in the maintenance man's place. "I recognize these. They definitely belong to our victim."

Madison took a sip of her bottled beer and leaned back on the couch. "Yeah, I thought the same thing. Apparently, whoever dispersed her belongings scattered them in several places. Not everything was in that dumpster. So how and where are her other things? There are still several items unaccounted for and I suspect those might have blood on them. Maybe that's why they weren't discarded in the complex dumpsters. Hell, they could be in a landfill by now. I'm going to ask Becca to do a mock up of Zoe's room based on the known items and see what we have missing."

"I hope you're not going to have her do that tonight, are you?"

"Of course not."

"Well, I know how you get when pieces start coming together. You don't stop."

"Am I that bad?"

He smiled at her. "No. You're that good. That's why we solve cases."

"I hope you're right, Josh. I want to bring justice for Zoe and put this guy away, so he doesn't bring such grief to another family."

"I have no doubt we'll get our guy or gal. Now, are you going to eat that other slice of pizza?" he said as he reached for her plate.

She slapped his hand. "Get your own. I'm eating all of this."

He jerked his hand back. "You never eat more than one slice."

She raised one eyebrow and slightly tucked her chin. "You think you know me so well, don't you? I have a lot of secrets that might surprise you."

He waggled his eyebrows and snickered. "I'll bet you do."

She hadn't planned on him staying that night. All she could think about was the case, but the more beers they shared and watched him strut around the place in those tight jeans, the more her mind drifted to spending time with him. He had become the distraction she had never planned on, and she hoped it wasn't interfering with her focus. *What the heck. The case can wait until tomorrow.* She slid over closer to him. "You going to sip that beer all night?"

"All night?"

Chapter Fourteen

Lightning was flashing, and the thunder was roaring. Sophie jumped up on the bed and squeezed between Madison and Josh. Her whole body was shaking. Josh reached under the covers and pulled Sophie next to him. "It's okay little girl."

Madison rolled over and smiled. "I turn my back, and you've got another woman in the bed with you."

He lifted the covers slightly. "She made the first move. What could I do?"

"You are such a pushover. Are you going to make the coffee while I shower?"

Josh looked down at Sophie nestled up against him and then back up at Madison. He pouted. "I can't leave her frightened."

She chuckled as she walked toward the kitchen. "Okay, I'll make the coffee, but you're going to have to take her outside soon, or you'll be changing my sheets."

He suddenly pulled back the covers. "Come on, girl. We've got to go outside." He jumped up, pulled up his jeans and picked her up. He carried her to the door, opened the French doors and walked out in the rain and set her down on the grass. The moment he put her down, she turned and dashed back into the house.

Madison walked into the living room as he was coming back from outside. He closed the doors and stood there drenched. "I took her out, but she …"

"Never mind. She'll use the potty pads. She doesn't like the thunder."

"Uh, do you think you could have mentioned that to me before I stood outside in the rain?"

She just laughed. "I guess your mother never told you not to play in the rain, huh?"

"Very funny. Forget the coffee. I've got to go home and change. I'll pick up some on the way. See you later." As the water dripped from the top of his nose, he leaned over and kissed her.

Madison fixed another cup of coffee and carried it into the bedroom. Sophie was curled up on the bed against the pillow. "You tricked him didn't you, girl?" Sophie just wagged her tail.

She finished getting ready for work, put plenty of potty pads down for Sophie, gathered up the photos and dashed to her car.

Becca was already at work when Madison arrived. She was in the back room putting on the last of the details on the board. "Looks good, Becca. I can see a clear timeline with each of our suspects. We're armed with more information than we had before; now I think it's time to interview our cast of characters again."

Becca heard the front door open. She crinkled her nose. "I think I'd better give him a hand. He's not real good at balancing the coffee."

Madison laughed and shook her head.

Becca greeted Josh at the door and immediately took the carton with the coffee. Then she saw the box of donuts and grinned. *I guess they had another sleepover.*

"You seem happy about something this morning."

"Guess I am. Ms. Hart is in the back."

"She's going to go crossed-eyed if she keeps staring at that board. I just completed updating it."

"Well, we might have more to add," he gestured as he made his way down the hall.

She followed him to the back with the coffees. "Oh?"

Josh set the donuts down on the table and turned to look at Becca. Becca smiled and winked. "So Detective Logan says we might have more to add to the board?"

While Madison laid out the photos, Josh reported what the old lady told him the day before. "I think I'm going to drive around today and see if I can spot anything that might look like the vehicle she described."

"Boss, I could do that for you. I'm sure you have more important leads to follow then to drive around looking for a truck. It can't be that difficult."

Madison sat down and folded her hands under her chin. She cocked her head to one side, glanced up a Josh, who shrugged his shoulders. "Okay."

"Okay, I can, or okay, you're going to think about it?"

Madison grabbed a cake donut, since there weren't any powdered donuts in the box, and took a big bite. "You have all the addresses of our suspects, but whatever you do, do not engage in any conversation. This is just to see if there is a truck that might match the description of the one we're looking for. I don't want you to risk putting yourself in danger."

"I understand. I'm only looking, nothing else. I've got it."

Josh took a sip of coffee and added, "But if you *do* find the vehicle, call us."

"Hey, you two, I've got it. Do not engage!"

Becca opened the bottom drawer of her desk, got her purse and pulled out her sunglasses. Madison scratched the top of her head. "Becca, you do know it's raining outside, right?"

"Yes, but I'm going undercover."

Josh burst out laughing, and Madison just shook her head. "What a team. Now, I think we'd better interview some folks." She tugged at Josh's arm and dragged him out the door of the office and headed for the squad car. "You want me to drive?"

She opened the passenger side door. "We look more intimidating in the squad car."

"Okay, then. Who's first?"

"Let's start back at the beginning. Maybe Jon Smith will remember some detail that he didn't think were pertinent when we talked with him before he heard of Zoe's death. We are going down the line, one by one and reinterview the neighbors too. Now, maybe the neighbors will be more forthcoming knowing that someone in the area has been murdered. Also, I want to see if anyone of our suspects changes their story."

Josh started up the car. "My money is on the wacko. His obsession with Zoe was just a little too freaky. I'd like to know just where he was during the time her car was driven to the airport."

"Hopefully, we can get that from each of them and collaborate their time frame."

He backed out of the driveway and headed back to the apartment complex. They knocked on the door, but no one answered. Madison could have sworn she saw movement in the window as the walked up. She knocked again and still no one answered.

Josh turned around about to head to the car. "I guess he's not home."

Madison knocked one more time, and still no one came to the door. She placed her ear against the door. Josh whispered, "What are you doing?"

"I thought I saw someone inside as we walked up. She shrugged her shoulders. "I might have been wrong."

They walked back to the car. Madison kept glancing back to the apartment but saw nothing. "Alright, let's talk to your wacko stalker again."

"I'm telling you, Maddy. He looks good for it. He's crazy enough to kill her and believe he didn't. He talked like she was still alive. Maybe that's his way of dealing with killing her."

"Or, maybe, his act has everyone fooled and he thinks he's pulled one over on us. From what Becca found out about him, he has a genius IQ, which would go to reason that he could create a crazy persona."

Josh slapped the dashboard. "See, what did I tell you? I think he's our guy." Suddenly, his cell phone rang, but he didn't recognize the number. "Detective Logan."

"Detective, this is Bob at the lab. We got Agent Hart's results back on that hair sample. It is a match to your victim, Zoe McClain. We also tested the watch for blood but found nothing. Would you mind informing Agent Hart?"

Josh silently snarled. "I'll be glad to tell her. Thank you."

He jammed his finger into the off button on the car's Bluetooth. "That was *your* lab rat. He wanted me to tell Agent Hart that the results came back on the hair. It was Zoe's."

"What has you all twisted?"

His face turned blood red, and his hands clenched around the steering wheel with the grip of death. "It's the way he said it. 'Tell Agent Hart I got *her* results back.'

I'm the lead investigator on this murder case, and it's his job to inform me. He works for the Police Department, not you."

As Josh continued to rant, Madison sat quietly. *Something else is bothering him. He normally wouldn't get that hot over something so trivial.*

He pulled the car over to the side of the road. "Are you having trouble with me being the lead on this case? If so, just tell me."

She continued to sit and stare at him.

"Are you going to say anything?"

"Josh, I have no problem working with you, but apparently you're having trouble working with me. Maybe you'd be better off with another partner. This case is all that matters to me right now and should be all that matters to you too."

"Of course. I forgot. Nothing gets in the way of Agent Hart when she's on a case." He pulled back onto the road and sped off to Stephen Clark's place. Neither of them said another word the rest of the drive. When they arrived at Clark's home, they approached the door. Josh knocked on the door so hard; Madison thought his fist was going to break it down. "Josh, you need to focus."

He turned to her with his jaw clenched. "You interrogate your way, and I'll do it my way." His lips tightened. He was about to knock again when the door opened. "Detective Logan and Ms. Hart. Nice to see you again, won't you come in?" Mr. Clark motioned them into the house. The house seemed more cluttered than the last time they interviewed him. "How can I help you?" Josh looked at Madison, and she turned away. "We'd like to ask you a few more questions about your relationship with Ms. McClain," Josh asked.

Josh unbuttoned his jacket and loosened his tie. "I'd like to know more about how you met Ms. McClain."

"I met her on a dating site. We had so much in common. We liked the same type of music, we both enjoyed attending plays, and she liked the world of graphic art and it's heroes. That's why I knew she'd love going to the convention with me. She still hasn't gotten back to me, and the event is this coming weekend. I may have to give her another call."

Josh furrowed his eyebrows and glanced at Madison. Madison stepped up closer to Mr. Clark. "Mr. Clark, Zoe won't be going to the event with you."

He snapped at Madison. "Yes, she is. She said she would."

"Stephen, when did Zoe say she would go?"

He dropped one shoulder and kept shifting his eyes between several areas in the room and fidgeting with the paper he was holding. "When we chatted online, she once mentioned she thought that was cool, and I sent her the invitation. She's been very busy with her teaching job. It may have just slipped her mind. I'll call her later."

Josh interjected. "So you have Zoe's number?"

"Of course I do. How did you think I would call her if I didn't?"

Madison looked over at Josh. He lowered his head and nodded. "Mr. Clark, Zoe is dead."

Clark started darting aimlessly around the room, shuffling his feet and screaming back at Madison. "Oh, no, she isn't. My Zoe wouldn't leave me. You're just trying to break us up like the others. I'll call her later, and she'll tell me that she's fine. I think you'd better leave now."

Josh slowly backed his way out as Madison left the room. Josh didn't take his eyes off of Clark. *He's in no condition now to talk with any further, but I'm not ruling this wacko out, just yet.* By the time Josh exited the house, Madison was already sitting in the car. He walked in front of the car to the driver's side hoping she would look up at him, but she kept her gaze out the window at the house.

Josh started up the car and headed back to Maitland. When he pulled up in front of the office, Madison got out and started for the front door. Josh backed out, and she hollered. "Aren't you coming in?"

"I have to update the Chief." Then he left her standing at the door. She took a long, deep breath and opened the door. There was no one in the office. It was still. Becca was most likely still doing her job looking for the truck. She slowly walked to the back and sat down and stared at the board. *Maybe working with Josh is just too much togetherness. I need to pull away for awhile and let him do his job.*

It was almost 3:00 p.m but the stress of what transpired between her and Josh had taken its toll on her. *This is why I don't like getting involved during a case. I'm not focused, and neither is he.*

She picked up the photos, left a note for Becca that she would be working from home the rest of the day and left. Sophie greeted her at the door wagging her tail. "Hey, girl. I'll bet you're ready to go outside." Sophie darted for the doors and sat waiting for Madison. Madison tossed her bag on the counter, and walked to the doors and opened them. Sophie meandered out on the patio and then sniffed her way through the grass looking for that perfect spot. Madison headed for the fridge. She wasn't hungry but pulled out a bottle of chilled Cabernet-Sauvignon that she'd been saving for her and Josh. She popped the cork out and poured a large glass and set it on the coffee table. She took off her clothes and put on her yoga pants and hoodie.

She didn't feel like leaving the house, and she sure didn't want to see anyone. When Sophie finished her ritual, Madison closed the doors and curled up on the couch. Her plan was to review the photos and spreadsheet that Becca had made for her reflecting what was on the board. She had broken her cardinal rule. She let her emotions trump the case. She was angry for allowing herself to get involved. *I thought it would be different since I wasn't on an FBI case, but it's not. It's who I am.* She took a sip of wine, then another until she had finished the glass. Without caring what time it was, she poured another glass and drank that as fast as the first. Her head was spinning faster than Sophie did when she greeted her at the door. She picked up the photos, but couldn't focus. All she saw was double of everything. She kept glancing at the clock. It was only 5:30 and she was wasted.

There was a knock on the door. Sophie ran to the door and sniffed, but didn't yelp. She staggered to the door and peeped out. It was Becca. She didn't want to see anyone but opened the door anyway. "Come on in. You want a glass of wine?" she slurred.

"No, thank you. I just wanted to update you. I thought you and Josh would be at the office. I waited but when neither of you showed up, it dawned on me your car was gone, so I figured you came home for something. "You look bad. What happened?"

"The hell with men. I should never have got involved with him. He's a jerk."

"I'm assuming you're referring to Detective Logan?"

"I am."

Madison could barely hold onto her wine glass as she stumbled her way back to the couch. "The hell with him. I don't need him to solve cases, or in my life. Now, what did you find out?" She plopped on the couch.

Becca sat in the overstuffed chair across from her. "I did find a truck that closely matched the description of the one the lady saw outside her apartment that night." She kept updating Madison on her day when she noticed that Madison had passed out. Becca locked the back door, covered Madison, put fresh water and food down for Sophie and let herself out the front door locking it behind her. *Wow, it must have been a whopper of a fight for her to feel that way. Where do they go from here?*

Pains shot through Madison's back as she tried rolling over. Suddenly she found herself on the floor next to the couch. Her head was throbbing and she was aching all over. *Crap! I must have fallen asleep on the couch.* She struggled to crawl back onto the couch. There was an empty wine glass on the coffee table. She looked around the room expecting to see Josh. *Did I dream he was here or was that someone else? I could have sworn I was having a conversation about what transpired yesterday. I need to go to bed.* She staggered into her bedroom, dropped her clothes on the floor and climbed into bed. It seemed like only minutes when her cell phone rang. She opened one eye, glanced at the clock. "What?" It was 8:30 a.m. She reached for her phone. "Hart"

"Boss, are you coming into work today?"

"Uh, yes. I'll be there in thirty minutes. Is Detective Logan already there too?"

There was a long pause. "No, he hasn't come in yet."

"Okay, I'll be there shortly."

She slid out of bed, shuffled into the bathroom and turned on the shower. She flicked on the light over the mirror. "Good Grief. It looks like I was at an all-night drunken party. Hell, I was, except I was the only one there."

She opened the shower door and let the hot water pulsate over her throbbing head. "I can't believe I did this. How much wine did I drink? Of course, I forgot to eat, that's why I feel so terrible."

She threw on her robe, pushed the start button on the coffee pot, let Sophie out the back and then dressed. The events from the day before began to flash before her and none so clear as her fight with Josh. She finished her first cup of coffee and called Sophie back into the house. "I've got to go. You be a good girl." She left wondering what was going to happen; would Josh come in, would he call, would he ask to be removed from the case...her mind was spinning.

Madison wasn't sure if Josh was going to show up, so she drove through McDonald's and picked up a couple of coffees for her and Becca. Turning onto Swoope Avenue, Madison took a deep breath as the office came into view. Josh was not there. "Okay, girl. You've got a job to do. He'll just have to get over it."

She opened the front door and called out to Becca. "Anyone here?"

"I'm back here, Boss."

Becca was updating the board. Madison set the coffee down on the table and stepped up to the board. "What's new?"

"Thanks for the coffee, but you might need both cups. I'm adding the information I found out yesterday that I told you about."

"What information? When did we talk?"

Becca put the dry-erase pen down and turned around. "You don't remember our conversation last night?"

"When was that?"

"Oh never mind. I guess you were tired. I drove to our suspect's homes and located one truck that came close to matching the truck the old lady described to Detective Logan. It was a Dodge pickup, but it was dark red with a single silver band along the bottom. However, it was a newer model, and there are so many trucks like that, I hesitate to say it was the one she saw. But you can check it out. I left a message with Betty at the Police Department for Detective Logan with the same information. She said she'd make sure he received the message the moment he comes in."

Becca never mentioned about how Madison blurted out about Josh. *I wonder if she remembers how angry she was with him? But far be it from me to bring it up, and besides, it was probably the wine speaking.*

Madison handed Becca a cup of coffee while focusing on the board. "Have you heard from Josh this morning?"

"Nope, not yet. He might be with the Chief?"

"What made you think that?"

"I know he likes to keep the Chief updated on what we're doing, and after all we found out yesterday, I assumed he'd meet with Chief Baker first thing in the morning."

"Yeah, that's probably where he is. So, where did you find the truck?"

"It was parked out front of David George's place."

"The ex-boyfriend. Interesting. He suggested he hadn't seen Zoe for quite some time. I think I'll have a talk with him today. Becca, do we have any aspirin around here? I've got a killer headache."

"Yes, I keep a bottle in the top drawer of my desk. I'll get you some."

"Thank you."

Becca left the room to get the aspirin while Madison studied the board.

Becca returned to the room just as Madison was about to add something to the board. "Thank you. I guess I'll let you add to the board. Josh says he can't read my writing, so it's best you're the one to update. We visited Mr. Clark yesterday. You remember our stalker? Josh questioned him, and he became extremely agitated. He's keeping something from us. But the weird thing was that he kept referring to Zoe in the present tense, and when I told him that she was dead, he flipped out. He's either completely wrapped up in his fantasy world of her and can't accept reality, or he's an incredible actor and was trying to throw us off. He mentioned that he met Zoe online. I'd like you to find out what site she visited and if she corresponded with any other potential dates. I'm going to drive out and talk to David George. If Detective Logan calls, you can tell him where I am."

Madison headed toward the front of the office to leave. Becca followed her to the door. "Boss, is everything alright?"

"Of course. Why wouldn't it be?"

"No reason. You just look a bit distracted today."

Madison lifted her head and stood up straight. "That's been the problem. I haven't made the case my primary focus, but that's about to change."

"Okay. But if you need to talk, my door is always open."

"Thanks, Becca, but I'm fine. Now, I need to get to work."

Becca watched as Madison drove off and then returned to her desk. She called Betty, over at the Police Station. "Hey, Betty, this is Becca. Are you busy?"

"No, why?"

"Ms. Hart wants me to check out the dating site and see if our victim was corresponding with anyone else. If you're not busy, could I swing by and use your computer access? Maybe between the two of us we can dig up her profile."

"Sounds great. You can come over anytime."

"Okay, I'll be there shortly."

Madison headed out of town to re-interview David George, the ex-boyfriend. She slammed her fist on the dashboard. "Damn, Josh, why did you have to act like such an ass? It just doesn't feel the same driving interview a suspect without you. I'd better suck it up. It doesn't look like we'll be riding together anymore. Shit! I thought this time it was going to work out."

She turned down the street where Mr.George lived and spotted the truck right away. "Close enough to the description. Now, let's see what he has to say."

She knocked on the door. "Good morning, Agent Hart. Have you found out any more about Zoe's murder?"

"We're working on it. I have a few more details I was hoping you could help me clear up. Do you have a few minutes?"

"Of course, come in."

Madison maneuvered her way through the piles of boxes. Mr. George lifted a heavy box from a chair. "You'll have to excuse the mess; I'm in the middle of packing up."

"Are you moving?"

"Yeah, I've accepted a position in Atlanta, and I'll be leaving next month."

"What kind of work do you do?"

"I'm a chemistry teacher."

Madison just nodded her head.

"Mr. George…"

"Please, call me David."

"Okay. David is that your pickup truck outside?"

"Yes, Why?"

"One of Zoe's neighbors reported seeing it at the complex a few days before Zoe's went missing. The last time we talked, you mentioned you hadn't seen her in weeks. Can you explain why your truck was at her place?"

He shook his head. "I forgot, I did go by and see her one evening. She called me and said she wanted to talk to me about something."

Madison observed his posture and demeanor as he shifted from side to side, suddenly looked down and would not make eye contact with her. She took the opportunity. "It seems strange that you could forget that you have talked with her since you were so concerned about your friend's disappearance."

He began to stutter. "I just forgot."

"What did you to talk about?"

He crossed his arms, "It was nothing."

"Well, the neighbor said the two of you were arguing. That doesn't seem like nothing to me, David."

David sat down hard in the chair across Madison. "I'm a bit embarrassed. But Zoe had been meeting people online, and when she told me about some of her dates, I became worried. That's what we were arguing about. It just didn't feel right for her to be going out with perfect strangers. There's no telling what can happen. She got upset with me and told me it was none of my business who she saw. She stormed off and that was the last time I saw her. I guess that's why I wasn't in such a hurry to call her back when she called me that night and left the message that she needed to talk to me. Now, I wish I had." He lowered his head and rubbed the back of his neck. "I should have called her and maybe this wouldn't have happened. Do you think someone she met online did that to her?"

Madison leaned forward in her chair. "Did she happen to mention any names?"

"No. But at that point I doubt she was going to tell me anything else. She was very upset, so I just left."

"And where did you say you were late Friday night?"

"I was having drinks with a few co-workers at Rocco's in Winter Park. I'll be happy to give you their names."

"Can you tell me what time you got home that night?"

"I'm not sure, but I can tell you I stayed until they closed."

She handed him a small spiral notepad and asked him to write down the names of those he was with on the night Zoe was murdered.

"You don't think I was involved with her death, do you? She was my best friend."

When he finished writing down the names, she reached across the coffee table, took the notepad, stood up and thanked him for his help. She didn't respond to his question, nor give any facial expression to his inquiry.

"We may need to talk to you again, but in the mean time if you can think of anything else you may have *forgotten* to tell us, please call." She walked to the door, and Mr. George followed. He was just about to close the door when Madison placed her hand on the door. "David, you might want to hold off on your move for now." Then she walked back to her car. Though she didn't look back directly at him, she watched him. He was leaning against the door frame with his hand over his forehead. *I guess that ought to give him something to think about.*

Chapter Fifteen

Josh dropped Madison off at her office and then sped away. His pulse was racing, and all he could think about was leaving before he said anything else. He started home, but when he turned onto Highway 17-92, he kept driving south. *Damn, why can't that woman show me some respect. Sure, she's an FBI agent and has had a great deal of training, but this is not my first time interrogating someone. I've solved nearly as many cases, if not more than she has in my career. Give me a little credit.* He ranted and raved the entire drive. Before he knew it, he had almost driven to Disney. "She's throwing me off my game. I can't think straight when I'm around her. Maybe it would be better if we weren't on top of each other the entire case. She's been doing it her way for so long that I doubt she'll yield. Okay, Detective, get over your ego, put your head back on straight, get to work and solve this case."

He turned around and headed back to Maitland. He passed her office, but she had gone. Even Becca's car was gone. "Ah hell, I might as well go home."

He swung open his front door and tossed his briefcase on the table in the foyer and headed for the kitchen. He jerked the fridge door open and grabbed a bottle of beer. Before he closed the door of the fridge, he had nearly finished that bottle. He reached in and grabbed another one.

He paced the living room reliving the argument he and Madison had. "What a jerk you are, Logan. She barely said a word and you totally went off on her. She was just doing her job. Okay, so she doesn't do it the way you want her to, but I doubt you're doing this case the way she wants to proceed either."

He finished the first beer and set the bottle on the coffee table and headed into his room. He stripped off his clothes and turned on the shower. He popped open the next beer and took a big swig and then set it on the sink before jumping into the shower. He let the hot water pulsate over his head and against his shoulders hoping it would relief some of his tension. "Oh, crap. This isn't going to change anything." He reached outside the shower, grabbed a towel and wrapped it around him.

I should go over there and apologize. He slipped into a pair of faded jeans and a navy-blue, tight fitting T-shirt. He grabbed his beer and started for the front door. "No. I'm not going to apologize."

He finished off another two beers before he fell asleep on the couch. When he awoke, it was nearly 8:00 a.m. His first thought was to drive by and pick up some bagels and coffee for Madison and Becca, but then he hesitated. *I don't guess she'll want to see my face this morning. I think I'll give her some space. There are other avenues of this investigation that I can look into without insisting we do it together. Who knows, we might get more done this way. I guess I'll update the Chief this morning on what we found out and then I'll visit one of our suspects. I'm sure she's already on the road doing her thing so I'm not going to call.*

He changed his clothes and drove over to the Police Station. *Hm, that's strange. I wonder why Becca's car is parked out front?*

He pulled around to the back and entered through the back door to avoid the reception area. He passed the Chief. "Chief, got a minute?"

"Sure. How's the case going?"

Josh opened his jacket. "I think we're making progress. That's what I wanted to talk to you about. I think at this stage in the investigation, it would better serve if Ms. Hart and I split up the interviews."

Chief Baker was standing at his desk. He placed his hands on the desk and leaned forward. "Is everything okay between you and Agent Hart?"

"Oh, fine. I just felt we'd cover more ground this way."

The Chief continued reached for a pile of papers. "Yeah, that sounds like a good idea."

Josh gave a tight-lipped smile. "Okay then. I'll get back to work."

He walked out to the reception area expecting to see Becca. "Hey, Betty, was that Becca Hamilton's car out front?"

"Yes. She came by to use our computer to do some research."

"What was she researching?"

"She was doing an in-depth background check on a few of the suspects in your case and also checking into the dating service that your victim had used. She was hoping to find out who else she was seeing."

"Did she find out anything?"

Betty looked over her reading glasses. "You haven't talked to Ms. Hart this morning have you?"

"I overslept, and I had another issue I was working on. I'll touch base with her later. Agent Hart wasn't here with Becca, then?"

"No. Becca said she drove out to talk with David George."

He nodded his head. "Oh yeah. I forgot about that," he mumbled as he walked out to his car. _She doesn't need me to do her job, but we would have discussed the interview before the incident yesterday. I blew it. Okay, Logan, focus on the case._ "Well, if anything comes up, text me."

"Sure will, Detective." She watched him walk down the back hall to the parking lot exit. _Was he trying to avoid seeing Becca or was it Ms. Hart? I think I missed something?_

Josh headed to his squad car with every intention of driving over to Madison's office, but couldn't bring himself to start the car. He thumbed through his briefcase as if he was looking for something specific. "I need some coffee. I might as well pick up some bagels too."

He kept glancing down at his phone hoping Madison would call, but the phone remained silent. He checked his text messages, which he had done only a half hour prior. There were no new texts from her or Becca. Swoope Avenue was just ahead, and there was Becca's car parked out front. The sweat began to roll down the back of his neck and his palms became sweaty. He parked as close to Becca's car as possible to give Madison plenty of room for her car in case she showed up while he was still there.

He took a big swallow of his coffee and marched up to the door, but before he could reach for the door knob, Becca swung open the door. "Good morning, Detective."

He swaggered in as though he was on top of the world. "I brought your coffee just the way you like it. Is Ms. Hart here yet?"

"Uh, she's has already headed out to interview Mr. George. I wasn't sure you were coming in today."

"Why wouldn't I?

"Well, you're usually here earlier than this, and Ms. Hart didn't mention you were going to be late."

"What *did* she say?"

"Not much. Only that she was going to interview one of your suspects. I assumed she called you."

He started for the back room and quickly changed the subject. "Nope. Anything new?"

"I updated the information Ms. Hart gave me from the interview you and she had with Mr. Clark. I did some checking on him with Betty this morning over at the station. This guy has been in and out of mental facilities most of his life. Supposedly, he lives with his mother, but I couldn't find any recent information on her. Didn't he say his mother had passed away?"

"I'm sure he said that she had lived there, but he eluded to the fact that she was deceased."

"I couldn't find any death certificate, but it was his mother that continually had him institutionalized."

"That's interesting. Have you relayed this information to Madison?"

"I was just about to."

"That's okay. I'll tell her."

"Detective Logan, is everything alright?"

"You're the second person to ask me that today. Do I look like something is wrong?"

"As a matter of fact, you do."

"What do you mean? Am I pale or do I look sick?"

"No." Becca hesitated for a moment. "It's just that when Ms. Hart came in today, she seemed like something was troubling her, and now you have that same look on your face."

Becca didn't mention what Madison said last night while she was drinking.

"I think it's the case. We're both under a lot of stress to find answers for the family and bring Zoe's murderer to justice. You know how involved she can get with a case."

"I sure do. That's why I try to do as much as I can to help."

"Becca, what time did she leave this morning?"

"She left as soon as we opened the office. It was about two hours ago. I expect her back any time now."

"I guess I'd better get to work." He started down the hall to recap what was on the board, and Becca returned to her desk.

Josh stood staring at the board but couldn't see what was there. All he could see was the look on Madison's face when he let her out of the car the day before. He breathed in a big breath, shook his head and tried to focus on the board. "Hey, Becca. When did this information come in about the truck?"

Becca walked to the back and beamed. "That's what I found when I did my *undercover* work. I found a truck that nearly matched that described by the old lady at the complex."

"You have it under David George's name. Is that who the truck belonged to?"

"Yes, that's why Ms. Hart went out to talk to him."

He nodded and then headed out the front door without saying another word. He sped down the street in the direction of Mr. George's place. He hoped to get there before Madison left. He had a few questions of his own to ask David George. Chances were that by the time he got there, Madison would be gone and she was, and so was Mr. George. "Damn, we're a team. I should be with her on this case. That's what partners do." *She's all about the case, and if she found out anything, she would have called me.*

He turned around and started back to the office.

Madison arrived at the office just after Josh left. When she opened the door, Becca stood up and passed her. "Did Detective Logan come in?"

Madison crinkled her nose. "What?"

"He just left moments before you got here. I thought maybe he passed you coming in. Never mind. How did your talk with Mr. George go? Did he confess?"

Madison sighed. *Was Josh here?* "Uh, oh yes. He confessed to arguing with Zoe. You were right, it was his truck. Becca that saved me a lot of time, thanks."

She wanted to ask about Josh but pretended she wasn't interested. "I wish we could land something solid in this case and soon. This is when I get frustrated."

"Yeah. Detective Logan said the same thing."

"He did?"

"He looked like something was bothering him, and when I asked, he said you both were under a lot of stress to bring justice for Zoe and her family and find her killer. He's as passionate about his work as you are. I guess that's what makes you two such a good team."

Madison nodded her head. "Yeah, we both want to solve this one." *I guess I should call him.*

"Oh, he brought you some coffee and bagels. The coffee is probably still hot, and the bagels are in the back by the board. He spent a great deal of time studying the new information you had me add to the board this morning."

"You don't by any chance know where he's headed now, do you?"

Becca shook her head. "No, I didn't ask. I think he said he'd get back to you later."

"Thanks."

Madison sat down at the table and sipped her coffee. It was getting cold, but she didn't care. Josh had thought enough to bring her some, so maybe he's over what happened yesterday. She hoped so.

She laid out the pictures Denise had given her of Zoe's apartment before it was cleaned out. Then placed the pictures taken of the items found in Charlie Foster's place next to them. One by one she identified what belonged to Zoe, but there were still a few things missing, and none were found at Foster's or in any of the dumpsters at the complex. *Why wouldn't he take all of the items? Where are her other belongings? We're missing something and why can't I see it?*

Madison left the photos on the table. "Becca, I'm going out for awhile to clear my head. I'm missing a critical piece, and it's driving me nuts."

"Okay, Boss."

Madison pulled through McDonald's ordered a large black coffee and drove over to Lake Lily. She parked her car and strolled the path leading around the lake. She mumbled to herself as she continued her walk. "It's right in front of me, I know it. If only I could bounce this off of Josh, we could probably come up with it." She stopped on the bridge and stared out at the fountain in the middle of the lake. She listened to the ducks and geese squawking for squatting rights at various locations along the shore. There was just enough breeze that caught the mist from the fountain and caressed her face as she stood there. Madison closed her eyes and breathed in the moist air. She leaned over the railing watching a turtle struggle to climb onto a lily pad. "I should do this more often. I'm so busy looking for bodies and who put them there that I am missing all this. I spend so much time looking for ducktape and shovels that I'm missing the rainbows and unicorns or life. When *we* finish this case, I'm going to take some serious relaxation time."

"I think that's a great idea."

She spun around, and there stood Josh standing on the bridge behind her. "How did you know I was here?"

"I didn't. I just needed to clear my head, and this is where I always find the most peace, and it's with you."

A tear from the corner of her eye trickled down her cheek. He reached for her. "Maddy, I'm such a jerk."

She leaned into his chest and chuckled. "Yes, you are a jerk, but you're my jerk."

He lifted her chin, kissed her forehead, then her eyelids and drew her lips to his. "I am your jerk! I'm so sorry."

She wrapped her arms around him and returned his kiss. "I'm sorry too. Do you think us working together is too much?"

"It can be if we let it."

She smiled. "I miss working with you and not because of how I feel about you, but because we're a damn good team."

He looked into her eyes, grinned and wiggled one eyebrow. "Yes, we are. Now let's get back to doing the second best thing we do together."

"Did you bring anything to eat, I'm starving. I can't catch the bad guys on an empty stomach. Are you going to feed me first? Let's run by the office, I need to pick up those photos. I thought we could review them at lunch."

"That's my Maddy, right to the point."

Chapter Sixteen

Madison headed back to the office with Josh following close behind her in the squad car. She parked her car and waited for him. When they walked into the office, they expected to see Becca at her desk, but she wasn't there. "Becca," Madison called out.

"I'm back here, Boss."

She turned to Josh, "I wonder what she's up to? Nothing new has come in since I left."

"There's no telling with Becca," Josh replied as they headed to the case room.

Becca was frantically drawing on the other whiteboard. Madison stepped into the room and turned to see that Becca had drawn a mock-up of Zoe's bedroom based on the photos from Denise McClain. She had color coded all the items that had been located. Blue for the articles found in Charlie Foster's back room, yellow for items found in the dumpster and leaving the other items yet to be located blank.

Josh swung around to look at what Madison was staring at. "Holy crap, Becca. How did you do this?"

Becca never hesitated as she continue her project. "I saw the photos of Zoe's bedroom and the list of items on the board under Charlie Foster and thought a visual would give *us* a better perspective of what we need to look for."

Madison just shook her head and beamed. "I can't believe we didn't see the obvious, but seeing it in your drawing, it's very clear. I just might have to find someone else to answer the phones and put you to work as an investigator."

Josh blew out a big breath. "I guess I'd better go out and get you another coffee."

Becca kept drawing but blurted out. "Coffee? It's time for lunch, and I'm starving."

Madison turned to Josh and shrugged her shoulders. "You heard what the lady said. You'd better get us all something to eat. I have a feeling this case is about to get very interesting."

"You've got it. The usual Ladies?"

Madison nodded, but Becca kept up on working on her sketch. "Yep, that'll be fine. Could you ask them to put extra pickles on mine today?"

"Yes, ma'am."

Josh left and headed to Kappy's to pick up lunch.

Becca finished up and then stood back with her hands on her hips. "Looks like we have a white elephant in the room."

"It does indeed."

Becca turned to Madison and smiled. "You look a lot better. I take it everything is alright now?"

"Yeah."

"Good. What's the plan for the afternoon?"

"Not sure yet. Josh and I were planning to study the pictures, but your drawing has given a clear image of what we need to be looking for. I think we might go back to the Foster's place and see if we overlooked anything.

But with the way he had everything out in the open, I doubt he's the one we're looking for unless he's just plain stupid. Did you find out any more on the dating service?"

"I'm afraid not. When Betty and I called, they were less than forthcoming on giving out any information on their clients. Maybe your FBI badge will have more pull. Have you ruled out the guy she dated who installed her cable?"

"We haven't ruled anyone out yet. I still want to talk to Jon Smith's girlfriend. The last time we spoke to her she seemed very nervous and defensive, and I'd like to know why."

They heard the front door jiggling. Becca stuck her head out from the room and there was Josh trying to juggle a box of sandwiches and fries, and another box of soft drinks. She dashed to the door, opened it and caught the box of drinks just as he was about to drop them. "Detective Logan, I think we might want to put a small table outside the door for you to set things on. Then you won't have so much trouble trying to open this door."

"That's a good idea. This door always sticks when I'm bringing in food."

Madison bit her lower lip. "Yeah, that darn door."

Becca quickly turned away. Madison grabbed the bag of fries balancing on top of the sandwiches. "Did you invite a guest?"

"No, why?"

"You do know it's just the three of us, right?"

"Yes, but we didn't get any breakfast, and everyone said they were starving."

"You are absolutely correct; we did say that. Thank you."

Becca had placed napkins and paper plates on the table and set the drinks out. Madison opened the fries and poured them out on a plate, and Josh handed out the sandwiches. Becca took a sip of her Diet Dr. Pepper. "Well, what do you think?"

Josh took a big bite of his Italian Sub, and the slaw escaped out the end, dripping all over his plate. "Great job, Becca. Now we have a major piece missing and a reason to revisit our suspects."

Madison leaned over and dabbed his chin as the juice from his Sub dripped down. "Makes me wonder why we haven't located it. If someone disposed of it, does it contain the evidence we need to determine our murderer?"

Josh put his sandwich down, took a sip of his Coke and stood up. "Maybe she was killed in her room, and the reason we couldn't find any blood spatter is because a pillow was put over her head before he shot her."

"You're assuming it was a male, but it could have been a woman. Zoe was petite, and even a small woman could have carried her body to the car."

"Yeah, could be. Maybe we should have another talk with Smith's girlfriend."

Madison turned to Becca, and the two gave a slight smirk. "Great idea."

"Okay, you two. What was that about?" He looked down at his shirt expecting to see part of his sandwich on his chest.

"Oh, nothing. We were just talking about that before you got here. You know the old cliché… Great minds think alike."

Madison quickly redirected the conversation back to the case. "Let's see where we are at this point." She stepped up to the main board. "We have several potential suspects and an unsub. The last person we know who saw Zoe was David George. We know the two argued about her dating strangers she met online. He says they are just friends, but he might have harbored resentment after their breakup. She trusted him and would have let him in the apartment, and he's strong enough to carry her out. He could have easily disposed of the items in the dumpster late at night without anyone noticing. Then we have Charlie Foster, who ends up with many of her belongings. He has master keys to all the units and could have used his key; snuck in while she was sleeping, killed her, tossed the items to make it look like she just left in the middle of the night." She turned and sat down staring at the board.

Becca pointed to the board. "Yes, but he was seen retrieving items out of the dumpster."

"That could have been an afterthought, realizing he could use those to set up his rent-free space behind the complex. He might not be too bright, but he still could have killed her," Madison stated.

Josh shook his head, put his hands on hips. "My money is on the wacko stalker, Stephen Clark. He is delusional and believes he and Zoe were a couple. He could have approached her and she rebuked him, setting him into a rage. We know he can be provoked easily, and he's strong enough to subdue her. No, my bet is on him."

Becca pointed to Chris Adams name. "What about the cable installer? Didn't he say that he and Zoe had dated? We only have his word why they broke it off. She could have dumped him and he couldn't take rejection."

"Good point, Becca. But his background didn't indicate any violence. He seems to be an easy going guy who just happens to like a lot of women. He may be a jerk, but I don't get the feeling he'd kill over one woman. What are you thinking, Maddy?"

Madison leaned back in her chair with her hands folded over her head. She squinted as she glanced from one board to the next.

"I think before we rule anyone out, or in, I'd like to determine exactly where Zoe was murdered. If she was killed in her room, then we can rule out our wacko stalker because we know she would never have let him in. But if she were outside, he could very well have been lurking around and waiting to approach her. In the meantime, I'd like us to talk to the roommates girlfriend, Ginny Stapleton again. I have a hunch I'd like to explore."

Josh reached over the table and picked up his sandwich. "There she goes. Those wheels are spinning, but do you mind if I finish my lunch first?"

Becca laughed, and Madison raised one eyebrow. "Far be it from me to keep you from your meal. I sure wouldn't want you to pass out from being deprived of this nutritional food. Here, have some more French fries."

Josh grabbed a few fries and tossed them into the bag with his sandwich and raced to catch up with Madison. "Are you driving?"

"I thought since this is a murder investigation, we'd have more of an impact taking your squad car."

"I guess I can eat later." He threw the bag in the back seat, set his drink in the cup holder and strapped on his seatbelt. Madison was already settled in but watched as Josh made his getting into the car a major production. "Are you comfortable now?"

"Yep. Let's go."

She smiled as he pulled out of the parking lot. "Where to, Agent Hart?"

"I'd like to talk to Ginny Stapleton again. Do you have that evidence I asked you about?"

"No, I need to swing by the station. I have the other ones in the trunk. It won't take a minute. I think Betty has it ready for me."

"Good."

Josh jumped out of the car and darted into the station and was back out in less than five minutes. He was nearly out of breath running to the car. Madison snickered, "What took you so long?" He jerked back his head, "What? I wasn't in there more than a few minutes."

"I'm just kidding. Let's go."

Josh was glad to have Maddy with him again. It just wasn't the same checking on leads without her. *We do make a good team, and we're going to nail our killer, and we'll be doing it together. As it should be.*

"Detective Logan, I think you should take the lead in this interview."

"Because I'm so charming with the ladies?"

She raised her eyebrow. "Well, you do have a way of breaking down their resistance and getting them to say just what you want."

"Not always, but I'm working on it. Yeah, I'll run with this but I want you to jump in if you think of something. What was I thinking? Of course, you will."

Madison laughed. "As if you wouldn't? Okay, here's what I'd like to present to the girlfriend."

Madison laid out her hunch and plan, and Josh agreed. They knew she would be alone and would not have Jon there as her back up. Madison was hoping she would slip up and contradict her previous story while talking with Josh; then she would hone in on any discrepancy.

The girlfriend's car was in the driveway. No other vehicles were there. It was perfect.

Knock, Knock!

Ginny came to the door but didn't open it at first. Madison could see someone through the sheer curtains. Josh knocked again. The door slowly opened.

He stood in front of the door with his jacket casually unbuttoned. "Ms. Stapleton, we have a few more questions we'd like to ask you. Do you mind if we come in?"

She held onto to the door and did not open it completely. "I don't know what else I can tell you. I've told you everything I know. Jon and I were here that entire night his roommate went missing."

"Well, I just want to make sure we have everything clear so we can rule you out."

Her voice quivered slightly, and she leaned against the door frame. "Rule me out? Am I a suspect?"

"Of course not, but our Chief just wants to make sure we have everything correct so we can eliminate those involved in the case. I'm sure this won't take but a few minutes."

"Okay, but I can assure you that I don't know anything about that girl's death, and I know Jon doesn't either."

Josh just smiled. "May we come in?"

She opened the door and motioned for Josh and Madison to have a seat in the living room. "Would you like something to drink?"

Madison and Josh declined and took a seat on the couch. Ms. Stapleton sat down in a rocking chair across from them. Her knees were shaking, and she kept twisting her hair. "What is it you need to ask me that I haven't already answered?"

Josh leaned forward, "We'd like you to go over that weekend with us again from the moment Jon came over."

"I already did that once."

Josh gave a slight smile. "Yes, and we appreciate it, but often as time goes by, people will remember little details they had forgotten. We just want to make sure we don't leave anything out."

"Okay. Jon called me Friday evening to ask if I wanted him to pick up anything to eat before he came over and I asked him to bring a pizza. I didn't feel like cooking. I had a long day at work and just wanted to chill."

"What time did he come over?"

"I can't remember exactly, but it was dark outside so it must have been about 8:00 p.m. He was excited about the game on TV the next day, so he picked up some beer too. We had planned to stay in all weekend."

"Did he leave anytime that night for anything else?"

She suddenly stood up from the chair. "No. I told you that we were together the entire weekend. I know you're trying to blame Jon for what happened, but he couldn't have done anything to that girl. He was with me."

Madison stood and walked up to her and put her arm around Ginny's shoulder. "I know this is difficult for you, but we need your help so we can find who *really* killed that young lady and anything you can remember is helpful."

Ginny sat back down in her chair and took a deep breath. "I'm sorry, but this whole thing has been very hard on me."

Madison sat down and leaned toward Ginny. "How is Jon taking all this? It must be hard for him to go back to his apartment after what happened."

"He's having trouble sleeping there anymore. He spends more time here than at his apartment. He was counting on Zoe to help with the finances and now that she's gone, he can't seem to meet the bills. He's anxious lately. He put another ad in the paper for another roommate, but as soon as they find out it's the room of a murdered girl, they back out. I told him he could move his things in with me but he insists on staying there. I'm not sure how much longer he can afford to live in that place. I've been cleaning out a lot of my old stuff to make room for him. I imagine he'll have no choice now, but to move in with me if he can't find someone to share in the expenses."

Josh unbuttoned his jacket and pulled out a small plastic bag from his pocket. He laid the items out on the coffee table. "Ms. Stapleton, have you ever seen any of these items before?"

She pulled up closer and looked down at the table. "Do you mean, have I ever seen watches before?"

Josh moved the watches closer to her. "Have you ever seen any of these watches before?"

She turned to Madison and then back to Josh and then leaned back in her chair. "I don't think so. They all look alike to me."

Madison bit her lower lip, got up and walked to the other side of the table. "This is important, Ginny. Have you seen any of these watches before?" Madison handed them to Ms. Stapleton, one by one.

"No... No... No... No..." then she hesitated when Madison handed her the last watch.

She quickly placed it on the table. "I don't recognize any of these. Why are you asking about watches?"

Madison picked up the last watch again and handed it to Ginny. "You didn't answer me about this one. Ginny have you ever seen this watch before?

Ginny's lower lip began to quiver, and her eyes welled up with tears. She picked up the watch and stared at it. Her hands began to shake. With tears streaming down her cheeks, she looked up at Madison.

Madison put her hand on Ginny's shoulder and softly spoke. "You have seen this one, haven't you?"

All Ginny could do was nod her head. She put her head in her hands and wept. Madison glanced at Josh. Josh nodded his head. They waited for Ginny to compose herself somewhat and then Madison asked. "Where have you seen this one?"

Ginny lifted her head and handed the watch back to Madison. "It's the watch I gave Jon for his birthday last year. He always wears it. I noticed he hadn't been wearing it lately, and when I asked him, he said he lost it but was afraid to tell me."

Her whole body was shaking, and she cautiously asked, "Where did you find it?"

Josh stood up and retrieved the remaining watches. "I'm sorry this has upset you, but we needed your help. Thank you."

"Wait! You don't think Jon killed that woman. He couldn't have."

"We don't know who killed her, yet. But if he was with you the *entire* weekend, I guess he couldn't have, right?"

She lowered her head. "Right." She was holding something back.

Madison and Josh would leave her to think about what she had just discovered.

"Ginny, thank you for your help. If you can think of anything else, please call me, day or night," Madison said as she handed Ginny her card.

Ginny walked them to the door. Tears stained her cheeks, and her eyes were red and swollen. As soon as Madison and Josh left she closed the door. Madison could hear her crying again.

Josh whispered to Madison. "She knows a lot more than she's telling, but she's going to need some time to process all this. In the meantime, I'm going to have someone keeping an eye on her. If she confronts Jon, we don't know how he'll react. If he's our killer, it could push him over the edge. We need to tread lightly right now."

They sat in the squad car for a moment glancing back at the house. Madison could see Ginny pacing in the living room. "I have a feeling she'll be calling me soon. She's reliving every moment that weekend, trying to get her facts straight."

Josh grinned. "Your hunch paid off. Good work partner."

She tilted her head and smiled. "Why thank you, Detective. I sure could use some coffee now. Feel like buying a girl a drink?"

"I'd love to. Are we going back to the office?"

"Yes, why?"

"We don't want to go in empty handed. I'd better pick up Becca some too, or I'll have to face her wrath," he laughed.

"Good idea."

"Maddy, what made you think of showing her those watches?"

"I just had a hunch that the watch was a gift. It didn't look like one any of our suspects would buy for himself."

"But how did you know she would tell you?"

"She defended him so much; I believe she was trying to convince herself as much as she was trying to convince us. She tried too hard. I think she suspected he had something to do with Zoe's disappearance from the beginning, but because she cares for him, she couldn't allow her thoughts to entertain that concept. Do you remember the first time we interviewed her?"

"Yes, why?"

"She was just a little too adamant about establishing his alibi. Every time we drew the attention to Jon Smith, her right eye would twitch, and she'd fidget with her hair. She didn't want to believe. But now after identifying the watch, she's questioning everything. She may discover other discrepancies in his story."

"I just hope she doesn't confront him. I think he might become unhinged."

"Somehow, I don't think she will, at least not directly. I think she'll be more subtle. But I expect her to call us back and when she does, I have a few more questions for her to ponder about our Jon Smith if that is his real name."

Josh pulled into the drive-through at McDonalds and ordered three coffees and then drove to the office. Becca saw Josh carrying the cups and quickly opened the door. "Well, how did the interview go. Did she take the bait?"

Josh beamed. "Your boss is a genius. Ms. Stapleton did and she ID'd the watch as the one she bought Mr. Smith for his birthday."

"Did you tell her where you found it?"

Madison grabbed one of the coffees and handed it to Becca. "No, we wanted to see if she said anything to Mr.

Smith about the watch, and see what his explanation was, but we're sure it will rattle him knowing we found it. Now, he'll wonder where."

Becca took a sip of her coffee. "Ah, good idea. Get him trying to create a story that he'll stumble over. I get it. Thank you for the coffee."

Becca started to the back room. "Does this mean we are putting Mr. Smith to the top of *our* suspect list?"

Josh pulled out the watches and set them on the table. "Let's just say we're holding a spot for him. We still have to shake his alibi, and I think your boss just might have done that today."

Madison sat down while Becca proudly updated the board. So much had happened that day, and Madison was feeling the emotional effects. "I think we'll give Ms. Stapleton some time to mull over what she learned today. How about if we call it a day?"

Becca finished the board and turned to Madison. "Are you sure?"

"Yeah. Something tells me we're going to get real busy soon, so we could all use some rest. I'll see you early tomorrow. Okay, Becca?"

"Okay, Boss. See you tomorrow. Detective Logan, see you too?"

He smiled at Becca. "Yep. I'll make sure I get here early, with coffee and bagels."

Becca retrieved her purse from the bottom drawer of her desk and left. When Josh heard the door close, he started packing up his papers into his briefcase. "Well, it has been a long day, and I know you must be exhausted." He leaned over to give her a kiss on the cheek. He nearly fell over as she pulled him to her and returned a kiss only shared by lovers.

"Why don't we get a bottle of wine and some take-out and relax at my place tonight?"

"Are you sure?"

She raised her eyebrow and grinned. "Oh, I'm sure."

"Okay, but I have to run by the station and update the Chief. You don't need to come. I know you need to let Sophie out and feed her. I'll pick up something from Antonio's and a bottle of wine and see you in about an hour. Is that okay?"

"Yeah, that will be great. I'll see you later."

Josh started out the door when Madison hollered out, "Josh."

He turned to her. "Yes?"

"Thank you."

"For what?"

"For looking for me this morning."

He winked and closed the door.

Madison stood in front of the board like she had done so many times before, but this time she began to see the evidence formulating a scenario. She just needed to figure out if it was Jon Smith, then why did he do it? What was his motive, and why and how did he clear out the room without anyone seeing him? *Not tonight, Madison. Tonight you need to forget for a while. It will all be here waiting for you in the morning.*

She gathered her things and headed for her car, and not a moment too soon. The sky opened up to the typical Florida afternoon shower. The rain came down sudden and steady. She could smell the sweet fragrance of the earth as the rain soaked into the ground. In spite of the rain, the sun was still shining. *This is the only place I've ever experienced this. It brings back so many memories. Nature's way of cleansing.*

As soon as she opened the door of her place, Sophie was there to greet her doing her spinning in circles routine and then darted for the French doors. "I know you're not going to want to go out in the rain, but I'll open the door anyway." As soon as Madison opened the door, Sophie scurried out back and quickly did her business. She didn't linger in the yard like she normally did. Madison grabbed a towel and dried the little pup off. "I'll bet you're getting hungry, aren't you?" Sophie raced to the kitchen and gave a short yelp. Madison put her hands on her hips and shook her head. "I swear you understand what I say to you. Okay, I'm coming."

After she fed Sophie and put down fresh water, she headed for the shower. She still had some time before Josh would be there. She showered and slipped into her yoga pants and a tight fitting top.

She was barely dry when there was a knock on the door. Sophie ran to the door, sniffed at the threshold, yelped and started spinning circles. "Gee, I wonder who that could be?"

Madison couldn't get the door opened fast enough for Sophie to greet Josh. She darted out the door and jumped up for him to pet her. "Hi there. Did you miss me?"

Madison reached for the wine, "I think she likes you better than me. I might be getting jealous. You two do seem to have something going on."

"She's a good kisser," he said as he leaned down to pick Sophie up. She immediately gave him a big lick on his cheek. "Okay now, I've got to put you down so I don't drop this food."

Madison had already opened the wine. "What a day, huh?"

"I guess that's an understatement. Looks like we've finally got our suspect."

Madison didn't respond. She poured the wine and handed him a glass.

"Maddy, we do, don't we?"

"You know what I always say. I don't rule anyone out until we have *all* the facts."

"What's going on in that head of yours now?"

"Nothing that can't wait until tomorrow. Let's just have an evening without talking shop."

"That sounds good to me." He lifted his wine glass to hers. "Here's to a kick-ass team."

She chuckled and clanked her glass to his. "We do have a kick-ass team." She wanted to share her thoughts on the case but didn't want to ruin the moment.

Josh put his glass down and reached over and pulled her into his arms. "Are we good?"

She slowly closed her eyes, wrapped her arms around his neck and lifted her lips to his. "We're good."

Chapter Seventeen

The rain was beating down on the roof that morning. A perfect day to stay in bed, but Madison wanted to get to work. There was another avenue she wanted to pursue before they talked to Mr. Smith.

She turned over in bed and smiled. Josh was still sleeping soundly. She propped her head on the pillow and stared at this amazing man lying next to her. Not only was he the lover she had hoped for, but her partner in crime, so to speak. *Damn, we do make a good team, but we won't always be able to work together on cases. Then what? Will the excitement fade? Have I exposed too much of my weaknesses with him? Don't blow it, Madison, don't blow it.*

Josh began to stir. He opened his eyes and smiled. "Good morning, beautiful. What a nice sight to wake up to. Is the coffee ready?"

She grabbed a pillow and slammed it over his head. "Coffee? You have a naked woman next to you and you ask for coffee?"

He tossed the pillow off, grabbed her and flung her down on the bed on her back. "I can wait for the coffee."

Madison arose and walked into the kitchen to make a pot of coffee. She expected to see Josh coming out at any moment, but instead she heard the shower running. *That's a first.* She smiled and looked down at Sophie. "There's a man in our shower." Sophie ran to the bathroom, and then returned with Josh following wearing a towel around him. She burst out laughing. He quickly glanced down at himself. "What are you laughing at?"

All she could do was to point at Sophie, who was sitting erect at his feet looking up at him. He looked at Sophie, but couldn't see why she was laughing. "Am I missing something?"

"When I asked your little girlfriend if there was a man in our shower, Sophie darted to the bathroom and the next thing I see is her leading you out with a towel around you. She looked so proud when the two of you entered the room, as though she had found the man in the shower all by herself."

Josh looked down at the pup wagging her tail and staring up at him. He had to laugh too. "She does look proud of herself, doesn't she? I'd better get dressed. He turned back to the room.

By the time he returned the coffee was ready. She poured him a cup and topped her cup and pulled up a bar stool. "Josh, I was thinking about our case."

"Gee, that's a shock," he snickered.

"I'm serious. When you left the office yesterday, it started to rain, and it got me thinking."

"About what?"

"It was raining the night Zoe was murdered and all that weekend. I couldn't understand why everything was tossed in an open dumpster. What if our killer chose that dumpster because it remained open and would most likely destroy much of the evidence?"

"That makes sense."

"But?"

"I heard that but."

"But there is still a major item missing, and it wasn't in any of the dumpsters we checked. It wasn't clear to me until Becca drew the layout of Zoe's room. It's the elephant in the room, and no one saw it."

"I know what you're talking about; I was wondering the same thing. Where is it?"

Madison took a big sip of her coffee. "I'd like to go back to the Charlie Foster's place and look around. He has most everything else that was in the dumpster from her room. Let's see if he also has that."

Josh set his coffee cup down. "If he has it, then how did he dry it out? Or, did he take it before the other things were trashed?"

"We have several leads I'd like us to follow up on today. I'll meet you at the office in about a half hour."

Josh leaned over the counter and gave her a kiss on her forehead. "I'll see you soon." Then he left.

Madison took her shower, dressed, let Sophie out, put fresh water down and grabbed her purse. "See you later. You be a good girl." Sophie ran to the overstuffed chair, put her head on the armrest and wagged her tail as Madison left. *I hate leaving her every day. I wonder how she would do at the office. I'll talk to Becca about it sometime.*

She thought she was getting there early, but Becca's car was already there. "Good morning, Becca."

"Good morning, Boss."

Madison walked to her office in the back and put her things on her desk and then crossed the hall to the case room. Becca had already updated the board. Under Ginny Stapleton's name was the positive ID of the watch. Under Jon Smith was written, watch with a question mark. "Becca."

"Yes, Boss."

"You got a minute?"

Becca made her way to the back. "What's up?"

"I see you wrote the word, watch, under Mr. Smith. What's the question mark for?"

"Well, we only have the word of Ms. Stapleton that it's his watch. I thought you'd want more confirmation. Maybe having Mr. Smith verify it's his."

Madison smiled and nodded her head. "Good thinking. You're right, we only have her word for it, and she could be setting him up. We need to know more about their relationship. I'll talk to Josh about bringing him to the station for an interview. Thanks."

"Just doing my job, Boss," she grinned.

Becca must have seen Josh's car at my place this morning, yet she never mentioned it. Just then the front door of the office opened. Josh was doing his juggling act with the coffees. Becca grabbed the box of coffee cups and followed him to the back. She set them on the table, and Josh placed the box of donuts down.

Becca grinned and winked at Madison. "You brought donuts today."

"I did, but I remembered *not* to bring any with powdered sugar."

Madison chuckled as she reached for her coffee. "Okay, let's plan our strategy for today."

"That's our Ms. Hart, right to the point."

Madison stepped up to the board. "Becca added the watch, but we only have the word of Ms. Stapleton that she gave that watch to Smith."

Josh interrupted. "Why don't we call him into the station for another interview and present him with the watch?"

Becca looked up at Madison. "That's a great idea."

Madison bit her lower lip. "Okay, but I also would like to go back and check out Charlie Foster's place again and see what else we can find."

Josh reached for a chocolate covered donut. "I have a meeting with the chief this morning unrelated to this case, and I'll see about getting Smith to come in this afternoon. I'll call you as soon as I have confirmation. This ought to be interesting. I'm eager to hear him explain how his watch got into Zoe's car."

"Yeah, me too." She glanced back at Josh. "Why don't I run back to the shop at the apartment complex and have another look around while you're doing that, or do you want to come with me?"

"I know you can handle it on your own. Keep me posted on what you find and we'll touch base after my meeting this morning. I would like you to be with me for the interview with Smith."

"No problem. I have only one thing I'm looking for at Foster's. I'll call you if I find it. Becca, I'd like you to dig up all you can on Ms. Stapleton."

"Will do, Boss." Becca returned to her desk and immediately started making calls. "Hey, Betty, are you busy this morning?"

Josh left for his meeting with Chief Baker while Madison drove back to the apartment complex. It was still early. *Maybe Mr. Foster will still be in the shop.* She pulled her car up close to the entrance. The garage door was up and his golf cart was still parked outside. She heard hammering coming from inside and when she entered Foster swung around raising his hammer. She grabbed for her weapon but as soon as he saw it was Madison, he quickly put the hammer on the table. "Sorry, I guess with all that's been happening around here, I get a little jumpy."

She snapped the strap back over her weapon, making sure it was secured in her holster. "Yeah, I can only imagine, especially since you're here alone, all hours of the day and night."

"What are you doing back here? I've told you everything I know. I just want to move on. I'm sorry I ever got that junk out of the dumpster. I didn't know it belonged to someone who was murdered. Hell, I'll be glad to give it *all* back."

"I thought you gave everything to the officers when they collected it for evidence?"

"I did, at least I thought I did."

"What didn't you return?"

"I had tossed some of the papers and canceled checks in a bag and put them out back. I meant to put them in the trash, but this thing has me so rattled that I just left the bag."

"Where is it now?"

Foster walked out the back door of the shop and retrieved a black plastic bag and started to hand it to Madison. "Just set it down." She donned a pair of latex gloves and then lifted the bag. The rain had saturated everything inside. "Do you have another bag I can have?"

"Yeah, sure." He reached under the work bench and pulled out a box of garbage bags and handed her one. She placed the wet bag inside the new bag and hauled it to the back of her car and then returned to the shop.

Foster was standing there scratching the top of his head. "What do you want with all that junk?"

Madison did not respond. "Thank you. I was wondering if I could look around in your room again?"

"Shit, your guys stripped everything from my room. They even took the TV, but have at it." He motioned her toward the room, but she motioned him and followed him into the back. There was now an orange crate as a bed stand where once was Zoe's nightstand stood, an old wooden coke box he was using as a coffee table instead of Zoe's ornate coffee table. The only other thing in the room was a single bed and old halogen desk lamp. Not much of a living quarters.

Madison strolled around the room as though she was looking for something specific, and then turned and walked out. "Thank you, Mr. Foster." She walked out towards her car when Foster hollered out. "Is that it?"

She opened her car door and turned, "We'll be in touch if we have any other questions." She could see him out of the corner of her eye. He watched her get into the car and then turned, picked up his hammer and resumed his work. Didn't look like a man trying to hide anything. *I think we can cross him off our suspect list.*

She drove directly to the forensic lab and carried in the plastic bag.

"Good morning, Agent Hart. What do you have for me today?"

"Good morning to you too, Bob. But it's just Madison right now. I'd like you to see if there is anything in this bag that will help us with our case. I retrieved it from one of our suspects. However, he may have just been in the wrong place trying to better his living conditions. But this is full of papers he tossed. I'll have to warn you that it's been outside in the rain for awhile. I'm not even sure it contains anything of use, but I knew it there was, you'd be the person that would find it."

"Thank you for your confidence. How soon do you need it?"

"Well, as soon as you have the time. I think we're narrowing down our suspect pool, and something in here might give us a lead. I know you're busy, so whatever you can do to help me will be appreciated."

"For you, Agent Hart, I mean, Madison. I'll get to it after lunch. Will that be okay?"

She smiled. "You're a doll, Bob. Thanks. I'll call you later this afternoon?"

"I'll be here."

She left the lab, drove through McDonald's and picked up two cups of coffee. She wasn't expecting to see Josh until around lunch but knew Becca would be ready for another cup. She turned onto Swoope Avenue, but Becca's car was gone. *Wonder where she is?* She parked her car, unlocked the front door and headed to the back with the coffee. She was just about to set the coffee down when the front door opened.

"Hey, anyone here?"

It was Josh. "I'm back here."

He strutted down the hall. Madison was sipping on her coffee. He picked up the other coffee and took a big sip. "How did you know I was coming?"

She cocked her head and grinned. "I guess I'm just psychic."

"What did you find out this morning?"

She picked up the black erase pen and drew a big X across Charlie Foster and the information under his name and then completed it with another X. "We can cross him off of our suspect list."

"I take it you didn't find what you were looking for?"

"No, and I don't think he ever had possession of it. But I didn't come back empty-handed."

Josh looked around the room. "What else did you find?"

"Our Mr. Foster found some papers among the items he took out of the dumpster and tossed them, but lucky for us he never got rid of them completely. He bagged it all up and tossed it behind his building. It was wet from all the rain, but Bob said he'd go through it for me and will call when he gets it all sorted out."

"Oh, Bob."

She tilted her head toward him and batted her eyelashes.

"You are so bad, Agent Hart."

"I know, but you love it. Now, did you get a hold of Mr. Smith?"

"I just got out of the Chief's briefing. I haven't had time. I thought I'd call from here. Hey, I saw Becca at the station. She and Betty are up to something. They were hammering away at the computers at the front desk. Do you have her on another hunt?"

"As a matter of fact, I do. I asked if she could dig deeper into Ginny Stapleton's background."

"That's interesting. I thought her performance was a bit dramatic. What are you thinking?"

"Nothing. I just want us to have all the facts on our list of characters. I'd like to bring them into your house for a more formal interrogation. You know sitting in an interrogation room can be a bit unnerving for the guilty. I can get a better read on them when they under pressure. I hate to say it, but I don't think I like our stalker for this. He doesn't fit the profile of the type of person that could commit this crime."

"Yeah, the more I think about it, I agree. Are we ready to cross him off our list?"

She turned back to the board and drew only one X across Stephen Clark's name. "Almost. One more visit and a few more questions and I think we can eliminate him too."

"Maddy, I'm feeling good about our progress and so does the Chief. I updated him on what we've discovered, and he agrees. He believes we're about to crack this case and so do I. Once we find that one item, I think we'll have our crime scene established, and our murderer."

Madison remained quiet, staring at the board. Her gaze darted back and forth between two of the suspects. "Something isn't adding up here."

"What are you talking about? Did you hear what I just said about the case?"

She waved him off and continued studying the board. "Yeah, yeah, the chief is happy."

Josh stepped up beside her. "Okay, what am I not seeing here?"

"I'm not sure yet. Something about these clues looks a bit too easy. I don't like it when it seems clear. Something is hiding beneath them. There's a dark side to these secrets, and we have to find out what they are." She suddenly turned to him. "I'm getting hungry."

"Good grief, woman. I was ready for you to reveal the killer. What do you feel like eating? Do you want me to run out and grab something?"

"No, I want to get away from the board, change our environment and come back with fresh eyes."

"What about calling Mr. Smith into the station?"

She took his arm and led him out of the room. She flicked off the light and locked the door behind them. "We can ask him to come in after we have our lunch."

"Okay, what are you in the mood for?"

"Anything but bagels or donuts."

Chapter Eighteen

Becca and Betty wrapped up their investigation into Ginny Stapleton and had discovered some interesting things about her past. "Thank you for your help, Betty. I couldn't do this from our office, but with your resources I'm able to help Ms. Hart and Detective Logan."

"Anytime. I love doing this sort of thing, so feel free to run by again."

Madison's car was parked out front. Becca raced back to the office expecting to see Madison. She saw the two empty coffee cups in the back room. *I guess they have come and gone. They do make a good team.* She tossed the cups in the trash, wiped off the table and laid out the print-outs. She started toward the board when she saw the two names with Xs drawn across them, but only one had a double X. *Hmm, why does one have two when the other only has one?* "Oh, well." She wrote under Stapleton's name, the information she and Betty discovered. She stepped back with her hands on her hips. "Nice job, Investigator Hamilton, nice job." She looked at her watch; it was 1:00 p.m. and she hadn't had anything to eat since the donuts that morning. *I think I'll run out and grab a bite.* She grabbed her purse and left. She turned east on Swoope Avenue.

Madison and Josh were heading back to the office and turned onto Swoope. Josh squinted his eyes. "Isn't that Becca's car?"

"Looks like it. I wonder where she's going now?"

Josh pulled in next to Madison's car. "I guess she's off to lunch too."

As they entered the back, Josh looked at the board. "Well, it looks like your amateur sleuth has done it again." The board had been updated.

"I never doubted her. I sure have a treasure in that woman, but I think you're right."

He blurted out, "I'm right?"

"I might have to encourage her to get her P.I.'s license if she keeps this up. I don't want to lose her, though."

"I don't think you need to worry about that. She's not only loyal to you as her boss, but she's your friend. You two have a history. Now, let's see what she found out."

They stood in front of the board like two mannequins. They both had their hands on their hips, heads tilted to the same side, looking like they were in a trance.

Madison broke the silence. "Looks like our Miss Stapleton has a history of losing boyfriends, doesn't she?"

"Yep. Why don't we see what Mr. Smith has to say about all this? I'll give him a call and see if he'll come in."

"Good idea."

Madison stepped into her office while Josh called Mr. Smith. She closed her door to give him the space he needed to slip into his official persona. "Mr. Smith, this is Detective Logan with Maitland Police Department."

"Yes," he answered.

"We'd like you to come down to the station at your earliest convenience. We have a few things we need to clear up so that we can move forward in this case."

"I don't know anything more than I've already told you. I didn't know Zoe that well. She kept to herself."

"I understand. But some things have surfaced that we think you can help us with."

"Like what?"

"I'm not at liberty to discuss it over the phone. How soon can you get down to the station?"

"Uh, I guess I could be there in about an hour. Is this going to take long? I need to get to work soon."

"No. We should have this wrapped up quickly. Thank you for your help."

"Yeah, sure thing."

Josh hung up and pumped his fist in the air. "Okay, Maddy you can come out now."

She walked in and stroked Josh on the shoulder. "I loved how you lured him in. His curiosity got the best of him. He wants to know what we know."

"I can't wait to see the expression on his face when I place the watch on the table."

The front door opened, and Becca came in with a bag and a Diet Coke. Madison stuck her head out of the doorway. "We're back here."

Becca set her purse in the bottom drawer of her desk, set her sandwich bag down and carried her drink to the back. Madison and Josh were standing there waiting for her with Cheshire grins plastered across their faces. She lowered her head slightly, rolled her eyes, took a sip of her drink and then looked at them. "What?"

Madison raised her eyebrow. "Good job, P.I. Hamilton."

Becca's eyes widened, and the smile on her face was priceless. "Uh, thanks. But I was just doing what you asked me to."

"I think you did a little more than that. You got more information about her than I would have in a week of investigating."

"That's not true, but thank you for the compliment. I hope this helps."

Josh turned toward the board. "Oh, this helps."

Becca set her drink down and pointed to the names crossed off. "Have we eliminated these two from the pool?"

Madison nodded her head. "We no longer believe the maintenance man had anything to do with it, but we're reserving our findings for our stalker, thus only one X across his name at this time."

Becca glanced at Madison. "Should we leave the names up there?"

"Yes, because there may be something under their names that might crossover with one of the other suspects."

Becca stared at the remaining names on the board. "It appears we have two heavy contenders for the title of the killer. That's strange. I never even entertained the idea it could be either of them, but the evidence is mounting against both of them and based on what Betty and I discovered about Ms. Stapleton, my money is on her."

Josh furrowed his brow and leaned forward to the board. "Why do you think it's her?"

Becca bit the inside of her cheek. "I'm not saying it's her, but her past leaves a lot of doubt about her character, don't you think?"

Madison watched the two of them discussing the case and then stepped in. "It does present some questions. Maybe Mr. Smith will give us some insight when we talk to him."

Josh jerked his head back, pulled back the sleeve of his jacket to look at his watch. "Speaking of that, we've got to go." He motioned Madison to the door as he headed out of the room. Madison casually followed behind him giggling and shaking her head. She turned to Becca as she exited the room. "Good work. We need to talk soon."

Josh started up the squad car just as Madison sat down. "You in a hurry," she smiled."

"I am not so much in a hurry as I am eager to get this guy."

"Slow down there Detective. You're much better when you ease into it."

He swung his head toward her. "Are you talking about the case?"

"Of course, I am."

"Uh huh."

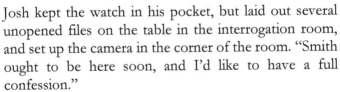

Josh kept the watch in his pocket, but laid out several unopened files on the table in the interrogation room, and set up the camera in the corner of the room. "Smith ought to be here soon, and I'd like to have a full confession."

Madison stood at the doorway. "You know that's not going to happen. I'd be satisfied, at this point, just to shake his alibi, or hers. I want to study his reactions to your questionings. I can tell quite a bit about a person by their body language, especially when they're being confronted."

Josh snickered. "Is that how you always figure me out?"

Madison smiled. "Oh, I have special tricks with you."

"Hey, I need to keep my focus on this interview. Don't be putting images in my mind."

Betty came down the hall, stepped up behind Madison. "Your guy is here. Do you want me to bring him back?"

Josh raised up from the table. "No thanks, we'll escort him back. Madison, you bring him in and tell him I'm with the Chief, but will be here in a minute."

Madison sauntered into the reception area wearing a gray pencil-stripped skirt, white blouse, and black heels and extended her hand. "Thank you for coming, Mr. Smith. This shouldn't take long to clear up a few things."

"Good. I'm not sure what help I can be."

"Oh, you'd be surprised. Sometimes the smallest detail can reveal quite a bit of information." She motioned him to the hallway. "We can wait for Detective Logan in here. He's with the Chief and should be in shortly. Can I get you something to drink?"

"Nah. I hope this isn't going to take to long. I need to get to work."

"It shouldn't." Madison walked over to the camera while Smith took a seat at the table.

Smith watched as Madison adjusted the camera. "What's with the camera?"

"Oh, we have to record all our interviews. It's here to protect those we question and make sure we're above board. You know all the new laws."

Smith began to squirm in his seat. "I could use a glass of water."

"No, problem." She hollered down the hall and asked Betty to bring a bottled water.

Betty came down the hall and handed her the bottled water, and immediately turned and left. Madison gave it to Smith. He tried twisting the cap off, but his hands were too sweaty. He reached for his shirt to use as leverage and finally opened it and then gulped several mouthfuls.

The unopened files lay in front of him. He kept glancing at Madison and then at the files. "How long is Detective Logan going to be?" Madison just shrugged her shoulders.

After about five minutes, Josh busted in the door holding another file. "Sorry about that. My chief wanted to update me on some information that just came to our attention." Josh sat across the table from Smith and opened the file he brought in. He furrowed his eyebrows, blew out his cheeks, then looked over at Madison and tilted his head.

Smith leaned over the table. His leg started to shake, and he was tapping his foot. "What do you need to ask me? I can't stay long."

Josh leaned back in his chair and stared at Smith for a moment. Then he pulled out his pen, opened his pad and set it on the table. "Can you go over the details of your whereabouts from the night Zoe went missing? I want to make sure we have all this correct."

Mr. Smith crossed his arms over his chest. "As I told you before, the last time I saw my roommate was the Wednesday before I left for my girlfriend's place. She stayed in her room most of the time. Friday I knocked on her door to tell her I was leaving, but she didn't respond. For all I know, she could have been gone by then."

Josh just stared at him. "What time did you leave for Ms. Stapleton's?"

"I'm not sure. I drove over to her place after work on Friday and stayed there the entire time, but I've told you this already."

"Did you, or Ms. Stapleton, ever leave the apartment that weekend for any amount of time?"

"No! I picked up pizza for the game. I didn't go home until late Sunday night. Neither of us ever left."

"Did you stay awake the entire time?"

"Of course not."

"How do you know she didn't leave while you were sleeping?"

Smith leaned back in his chair. "Are you suggesting that Ginny had something to do with this? She was jealous, but could never hurt someone."

Madison stepped up to the table. "I thought you said she was fine with you having Zoe as your roommate?"

"Uh...she was. But she gets a little possessive sometimes. She kept wanting me to move in with her. I finally had to break it off with her this week. She's too needy for me."

Madison glanced over at Josh and slightly nodded her head.

Josh took out the bag with the watch that Ginny identified as the one she gave Smith and placed it on the table. "Have you ever seen this watch?"

Perspiration started dripping from Smith's forehead. He reached over and picked up the watch. "No, it's not mine."

"Ms. Stapleton told us she gave it to you for your birthday last year."

"Well, she's lying. That is not my watch and she never gave it to me. She's just trying to get back at me for dumping her." Josh sat quietly and picked up one of the files, then looked up at Smith. "We have a problem, Mr. Smith. Your girlfriend swore the watch we found in Zoe McClain's car was yours.

Smith jumped up from his seat. "It's not my watch, and I've never been in her car. I think I want to speak to an attorney now."

Josh closed the file and slammed it on the table. "That's your right. But if you had nothing to do with this and can help us find who did, you could be hindering our investigation. That's not going to look good for you. You're free to go, but if I were you, I wouldn't be taking any trips for awhile."

Josh picked up the files, stood and started out of the room with Madison.

Smith hollered out as they reached the door. "Why don't you check Ginny's alibi. I was sleeping most of the weekend and cannot vouch for her. She was jealous as hell of Zoe and wanted me to get rid of her."

Josh closed the door and gave Madison a thumbs up. They walked back into his office. Betty called back to him to let him know that Mr. Smith had left. Madison turned to Josh. "He's scared."

"He is. I wonder what his next move will be. I'll bet he confronts Ginny, which will put her on the defensive too. We need to keep the pressure up until one of them caves."

"Nice work, Detective."

"Why thank you, Agent Hart. Can I buy you dinner tonight to celebrate?"

"Let's not be celebrating until we have our killer or killers behind bars, but you can buy me dinner and a glass of wine. And tomorrow we'll have another go at Stapleton. Her past may be catching up to her."

"Are you suggesting they are in it together?"

"I'm not suggesting anything, but I'm not ruling it out either."

They drove back to the office and found Becca at work. "Becca, you should have gone home by now. It's late."

"I've been on the edge of my seat. I wanted to know how the interrogation went. Did he confess?"

Madison grinned. "No. He asked for his attorney, but not before he revealed some pertinent leads. He denied owning the watch for one and then said he broke up with Ms. Stapleton. He also let it slip that she wanted him to get rid of Zoe and get another roommate, or better yet move in with her. But the best part was he told us he was sleeping most of the weekend and couldn't vouch for his ex-girlfriend's whereabouts. It seems like both their alibis are crumbling."

Becca's eyes widened. "What's next?"

"What's next is that you go home and get some rest. We're all going to need to be at the top of our game. I feel something is going to bust wide open soon."

Becca pulled her purse out of her desk drawer. "Do you want me to update the board first?"

"Nah, you can do that in the morning. Have a restful evening and I'll see you tomorrow."

"You've got it, Boss."

Josh watched as Becca drove off. "Do you think she's ever going to call you Madison at work?"

"Is Betty ever going to call you Josh at the station?"

Josh chuckled. "Fat chance. Point made. But aren't you two friends at home?"

"We are, and she calls me Madison outside the office."

Josh shook his head. "I guess I should call you Ms. Hart while we're working."

"I don't think so," she whispered as she kissed him on the cheek.

"Okay, where would you like to dine this evening?"

"Antonio's"

"I thought we weren't celebrating?"

"Not the case."

Josh smiled and opened the door for her.

When they arrived at Antonio's they chose a table on the balcony overlooking Lake Lily and ordered a bottle of wine. Josh looked across the table at her. "Do you remember the first time we came here?"

"I do. We had just finished our first case together. Funny, though, I didn't think at the time that I would be staying. I figured we'd wrap up the case, and I would be back in DC with the FBI."

The waiter brought out a bottle of Cabernet Sauvignon. Josh took the bottle and poured a glass for Madison and then himself. He set the bottle on the table and lifted his glass. "Here's to the FBI and my partner."

She lifted her glass. "I'll drink to that."

They finished their meal and wine. "You feel like listening to some music by the lake?"

She reached over and took his hand. "Not tonight, but I'll take a rain check. I'm very tired and exhausted, and I have a feeling tomorrow is going to be hectic. Do you mind just taking me to get my car?"

"Sure. Are you alright?"

"Just tired. Nothing that good nights sleep won't cure."

He drove her back to the office. He walked her to the car and kissed her goodnight. "See you in the morning."

"Sounds great. Why don't you swing by for coffee at my place before we go the office?"

"Do you want me to bring some bagels?"

"That would be fine."

She drove down the street and turned into the complex. Josh sat in his car watching her until her car was out of sight and then went home.

He pulled into his place, opened the front door and tossed his briefcase on the table. He looked around at the empty home. *I would love to share this place with her, but I doubt she's ready, or will ever be for that matter. She's one of the most independent women I know. I don't want to scare her off. It just dawned on me that she has never even asked me about where I lived or how I lived.*

He showered and grabbed a beer out of the fridge and walked out on the back patio overlooking Lake Minnehaha. The moon was reflecting on the water as it shimmered across the top of the waves made by the wake from the boats. "Damn, I would love to share this with Maddy. Maybe when this case is done, and we have a little down time, I'll approach her with a dinner invitation here at home. I could invite her sister and Cole too, so she wouldn't feel ambushed. Good grief, man, what are you afraid of?" *I'm afraid she'll turn and run.*

He finished his beer and went upstairs. He opened the French doors of the bedroom balcony to feel the night air as he slept. He looked over the massive back yard. "There would be plenty of room for Sophie to play. Quit dreaming and go to bed."

Josh jumped out of bed the next morning, showered, dressed, and raced to over to Madison's. He knocked on the door, but there was no answer. He knocked again and still no answer. He could hear Sophie whimpering on the other side of the door. He pulled out his cell and called her.

"Hello," she said in a weak voice.

"Maddy, are you okay?"

"What time is it?"

"It's 8:00 a.m."

"Are you coming over?"

"I'm at the front door."

She hung up and stumbled to the door and opened it. Sophie darted out to greet Josh.

"Woman, you don't look too well."

"I have a terrible headache."

"You didn't have that much wine last night. Do you think you ought to see a doctor?"

"No. Let me take a shower, and I'll meet you at the office. Would you pick up some coffee and make mine strong," she said walking back to her room. Sophie raced to the patio doors.

Josh opened the doors for Sophie to go out. He hesitate for a moment debating whether he should wait for her, but opted to leave the door ajar for Sophie and then he left.

He drove to the office. Becca was already there in the back room updating the board. She turned when she saw him come in. He only had the bag of bagels. "No coffee this morning?"

"Oh, crap. I'll be right back."

When he returned with the coffee Becca was munching on a bagel. "Bagels today, huh?"

He tilted his head. "Did you want something else?"

"No, bagels are fine. Is Ms. Hart with you?"

"She should be coming in soon. Thanks for reminding me about the coffee."

Becca continued with working. "I guess she'll be crossing off some of these other suspects now."

"You know Maddy, she won't cross them off until she's positive she can exclude them. But when she does, she'll be honing in on the rest until she's weeded out all but the killer. She has a drive like no one I've ever met in the business. She's a damn good investigator."

"She sure is. I hope to be as good as her some day."

"Ah, you have aspirations of becoming a P.I.?"

"Well, you two keep telling me I should. I just might. I've learned a lot from her, and she encourages me to step out more. Of course, I would never leave her."

"She would hate to lose you, but being a private investigator could be another asset you bring to the table. God, knows she appreciates what you do for her now."

"Who appreciates whom?" They heard coming up the hall.

"Good morning, Boss."

"How's your head?"

"Fine, now who were you both talking about?" she asked as she reached for a cup of coffee.

Josh got the message and didn't say another word about how she was feeling, at least not in front of anyone.

"I was just telling Becca what a great job she done helping us with the case."

"Josh is right, Becca. I don't know what I'd do without you. Now, how's our case looking this morning?"

Becca turned to the board. "I was just asking Detective Logan if you were ready to cross off any other names."

"Well, Detective Logan. What do you think?"

"It's your board."

"Yes, but it's *our* case."

Josh walked up to the board, picked up a marker and drew another X across Stephen Clark's name. "Okay, how do we like the cable guy?"

Madison hesitated for a moment. "I don't think he's our guy either, but let's put a single X across his name, and the same with the ex-boyfriend, David George. That narrows it down so we can concentrate on our primaries. I think we need to talk to Ms. Stapleton again. Her story is not adding up."

Josh took a sip of his coffee. I wonder how she's going to respond to the accusations of her ex-boyfriend. Not well, I suppose. Based on other relationships she's had, I imagine she's going be very explosive."

"Are you ready to see what else she'll have to say now?"

"Let's do it. I'll call her into the station."

Josh pulled out his cell phone and made the call. "Ms. Stapleton, this is Detective Logan. We talked yesterday. We'd like you to come down to the Maitland Police Station; we have just a few more questions we need to clear up. How soon can you get here?"

"I don't know why I have to come down there. I told you everything yesterday. I just want to move forward. Is this going to take long?"

"No ma'am. We should have all we need from you this afternoon. With what Mr. Smith told us yesterday and your information, we think we can settle this as soon as we talk to you."

"Mr. Smith? Was Jon there? What did he say?"

"We'll discuss that with you when you get here."

"Okay. I'll be there in about an hour. Is that alright?"

"That will be fine. Thank you." Josh quickly hung up.

Madison was just about to ask him what she said when her cell rang. "Good morning Ms. Hart, this is Bob at the lab. I have a few interesting things I was able to find from the items in the trash bag."

"Thanks, Bob. I'll be right there."

"Bob? Your new squeeze?" he chuckled.

"Yes. He found something in the trash. You go ahead, and I'll see what he's found and meet you at the station later."

Josh headed to meet Ms. Stapleton and Madison to the lab.

She pulled up to the back door of the forensic lab. "Thanks for calling, Bob. What do you have?"

"Well, everything was pretty wet, but I was able to pull out a few documents and some canceled checks. I found a note I thought was interesting. It looks like your victim wrote it."

Madison donned her gloves and cautiously picked up the note and started reading it.

> Jon,
>
> *I'm beginning to feel uncomfortable with you just showing up in my room anytime you, please. I'd appreciate it if when you see my door closed you would knock instead of just coming in.*

I told you I would pay you every month, and I've never been late, so you don't need to come in and ask me when I'm going to pay you. I understand you're under financial difficulties at this time, but that is not my problem.

If your intrusions continue, I'm going to be forced to find another place to live.

Zoe

Madison took a long deep breath. "That sounds like motive to me."

"That's what I thought when I read it. Also, I have a print out of some canceled checks."

"Thanks, Bob. I appreciate your putting a rush on this. This is going to be a big help." She turned to leave when he called out to her.

"That's not all."

She turned. "There's more?"

"As I was looking at the canceled check something didn't seem right, so I compared the signature with the note and they didn't match. Someone else wrote those checks."

Madison widened her eyes. "Interesting! I think I'll check with her bank records."

She left with the new information and headed for the station. Josh was already there and Ginny's car was parked out front. She raced inside. "Hey Betty. How long has Ms. Stapleton been in there with Josh?"

"She just arrived."

Madison darted down the hall and opened the interrogation room. She stepped up behind Josh and whispered what she found out. She pulled up a chair next to Josh and then let him proceed.

"As you know we talked with Mr. Smith yesterday. However, his account of your weekend was quite different than yours."

"What did he say we did?"

"He cannot account for where you were because he said he slept most of the weekend."

"That's not true. It was me who slept a lot. I had a migraine headache and spent much of the time in my room with the curtains drawn and a cold pack over my head."

"He also denies that you gave him that watch. He told Agent Hart that he had never seen that watch before and that you are just upset with him for *dumping* you."

"Dumping me? If you want to know the truth, I kicked him out. I couldn't tell you if he stayed at my place that weekend or not. I do know he was upset with his roommate. He said she hadn't paid him everything she owed, and he was getting frustrated with her making excuses. He said he was going to have to ask her to leave. He wanted to find someone more reliable."

Madison leaned across the table. "Ginny, was Jon having an affair with Zoe McClain?"

"Of course not! He didn't even like her that much. He just needed the money."

Madison laid the note sealed in a clear plastic bag on the table and slid it over to Ginny. She picked it up and read it. "That bastard. I knew he was hiding something. He's been acting strange ever since she disappeared. I should have kicked his ass out long before now, and to think I lent him money to get by. You don't think he killed her, though, do you?"

Madison took the note from her and placed it back into a file. "Ginny, could you write down your updated version of what happened that weekend for me?" she handed Ginny a large yellow pad and pen.

"Sure. You can't trust any of them."

"Any of them?" Josh asked.

"Any of you men," she snarled.

Madison and Josh waited until she completed her new version of what happened. Madison took the pad and left the room, but Josh remained.

When she returned a few minutes later, she glanced at Josh and gently shook her head. "Ms. Stapleton, you can go now but please don't leave the area. We may need to talk to you again."

She dropped her head in her hands and started to bawl, and then immediately stopped, got up, ran her fingers through her hair and left the room without saying a word.

Josh looked over at Madison and shrugged his shoulders. "That was odd."

"It sure was."

"It seems these two cannot get their stories straight. Either one of them could be our murderer."

Madison leaned against the doorway. Her face became pale and her knees buckled from under her. Josh dashed to her side just as she was about to collapse. "Okay, this is something more than a simple headache."

"Seriously, Josh. I think I'm just exhausted. You always say I put too much into a case. I want to get Zoe's bank records and see how she spent her money. It might be she confronted whoever was writing checks on her account. "

"I can have Betty do that. You need to get some rest. I'm taking you home. We can get your car later."

"I'm not going home…"

"Don't argue with me Ms. Hart. I think I'm capable of getting the bank records, and if anything looks fishy, I'll call you. Now get that pretty butt of yours in my car."

She was too exhausted to argue with him. Her legs felt wobbly and her balance wasn't good. She leaned on his arm as they went out the back door. He opened the passenger side of his car and helped her in. *I don't like seeing her like this.* He drove her to her place and walked her back to her bedroom. He helped her undress and into bed. She turned to him. "I'm so sorry. I guess I just need to sleep." She turned her head and immediately drifted off to sleep. Sophie jumped up on the bed and snuggled next to Madison. "You stay with your mommy, little girl, and I'll be back later to let you out." Sophie looked up at him and slightly wagged her tail.

Josh let himself out and locked the door. He drove over to the office to inform Becca. She was on the phone when he arrived, so he stood and waited. She hung up and looked up at him. "What's wrong? It's written all over your face. Is Madison okay?"

That was the first time he had ever heard her call Madison by her first name. "I just took her home. I think she's doing it again. She tries to hide it, but the case is getting to her. Do you have a key to her place?"

"As a matter of fact I do. She gave me one in case she couldn't get back in time to let Sophie out. Should I go and stay with her?"

"I don't think that's necessary. I just want to make sure she's okay. I'm going to check out a few things. I'll keep you posted, but unless it's critical, I don't want to disturb her. I'm going back there this evening and check on her. If she calls you, would you please let me know?"

"Of course I will. Is there anything I can do from here?"

"Not yet."

"I forgot to ask, how did the interview go this morning?"

"Let's just say the dynamics between that couple were revealing. One of them is not telling the truth, and the other one is holding back. Maybe after a check of Zoe's bank records, we can find out. I'm heading there now. I'm not sure I'll be back before morning so if you don't hear from me, I know Madison will want you to go home and rest too."

"Okay, but you have my number. If there is anything I can do, don't hesitate to call me."

He nodded and left for the bank.

Madison fell into a deep sleep, but her body tossed and turned. Her dreams were tangent fragments of the case. She saw Zoe pointing to something, and then a large figure carrying what looked like a body out the back door of her apartment and carefully placing it into the trunk of Zoe's car. The next scene was a tall, dark figure rummaging through the drawers in Zoe's dresser and bagging up everything into large garbage bags. All the evidence was forming her dream. She finally awoke with perspiration was running down her back. Sophie was lying on the bed just staring at her. "I'm okay, girl." The clock said it was nearly 5:00 p.m. "Crap, I've slept the whole day." She checked her voice mail and text, but there was nothing from Josh. "If he found anything he would have informed me. I might as well rest." Her head no longer hurt, and she felt a little more refreshed, but the day was wrapping up with no new leads. Josh would contact her if something came up.

She leaned down to pet Sophie. "You want to go outside?" Sophie remained on the bed. *That's strange.* She walked into the kitchen for a glass of water and saw a note on the counter.

> *Maddy,*
>
> *I picked up some Wonton soup. Mom always said chicken soup can cure anything, but I didn't know where to get any chicken soup, but this broth is chicken stock. I left some in the fridge for you. I'll call if there's anything new.*
> *Josh*

She opened the fridge to a container of soup. She heated it in the microwave and poured it into a mug. "Perfect. What a guy. Why do I treat him so badly? Being badly burned once can leave a scar that's hard to ignore." She finished her soup and returned to her bed.

Betty had the subpoena for Zoe's account ready for Josh. She called ahead to the Wells Fargo on 436 to inform the branch manager that Detective Logan was on his way. He arrived within ten minutes of the call with the subpoena. The branch manager greeted him and escorted him into her office. "What is it you're looking for, Detective?"

"I'm not sure, but this is the young woman who was murdered."

She slapped her hand over her mouth. "The one they found at the airport?"

"Yes."

"That's just awful. Have you arrested anyone yet?"

"We're close. May I see the records?"

"Oh, yes. How far back do you want me to go?"

"Three months, and I want a copy of the checks she's written to date."

"No problem. I'll get those for you right now." She left the room and returned with a stack of papers. "This is all we have right up to last week."

"Last week?"

"I guess some of the checks didn't get cashed until then. That's not uncommon for people to hold off depositing or cashing them." She handed him the documents. "Is that all you'll need from us?"

"Thank you. That's all for now."

It was almost 5:00 p.m. He stopped at the Chinese take-out and ordered Madison some Wonton soup. He lightly knocked on her door, but there was no answer. He let himself into a waiting little pup spinning in circles at his feet. He leaned down and whispered. "How's your mommy?" Sophie darted for the back. He hesitated and slowly walked to the doorway of her bedroom. She was sound asleep. He motioned Sophie to come out. He let her outside while he wrote Madison a note and then put the soup in the fridge. When Sophie came back in, he closed the French doors and quietly left.

He swung by and ordered pizza to go at Antonio's. His plan was to stay up and study the bank statements while he ate, but after he had undressed, drank a bottle of beer, he lay on the couch and fell asleep.

Josh tossed and turned on the couch until he rolled off onto the floor. "Crap." The box of pizza flipped over on top of him. He tossed the remaining pizza back in the box and headed for bed, but he couldn't sleep.

After about an hour, he got up and showered. He laid the bank records across the table and methodically went through every item. Her expenditures weren't unusual for a young woman. Her bills had been paid, she purchased a new outfit, and paid her groceries and gas. When he got to the time frame when she moved in there were the typical items purchased for her room. One item stood out. She ordered a brand new bed and mattress. *Hmm, that's what Madison said was missing. But now we have a make and model. She'll be glad to follow up on that since we never located any of the other items that were still missing. I'll bet that mattress has the blood evidence we need.*

He continued through the pages until suddenly Zoe's expenses changed, all coinciding with the time just before her death. There were several checks written out for large amounts of cash. Suddenly, he jerked his head back and pulled the paper up as close as he could studying the canceled checks. He raced to his briefcase and pulled out the note written by Zoe. He held them side by side. "This is *not* her signature." Then he brought his attention to the dates. "These checks are signed by Zoe after her death. He rummaged through his case looking for the hand-written account by Ginny Stapleton. "Just what I thought." He looked at the clock in the kitchen; it was only 4:00 a.m. He tossed everything back in his briefcase and got dressed.

He hurried to his car. There wouldn't be anyone but the night shift at the station and that would give him time to review all they had on the case without interruption. He reached inside his pants pocket for his keys and discovered he still had Madison's car keys and the keys to her office. "This is even better." He pulled through the drive-through and ordered two large black coffees, and then headed for Madison's office.

It was pitch dark outside, and no one would be bothering him for several hours. The case board would be all his. He unlocked the door and locked it behind him. He took all the papers and spread them on the table. Josh kept switching his glance between the papers on the table and the board. "Damn, this must feel the way Madison feels when she's onto something." He checked his watch several times. He stood in front of the board and drew another X across the cable guy and the ex-boyfriend. "They had nothing to do with this," he said aloud.

He stood back again with his hands on his hips. "We've got you now, you son-of-bitch."

It was all he could do not to call Madison and share his excitement with her, but she needed her rest. He started pacing the room and repeatedly looking at his watch. He grabbed one of the cups of coffee and darted out the front door, leaving everything in the back room. He locked the door, jumped in his car and sped off. He raced down Highway 17-92 to the apartment. He didn't want Mr. Smith to leave for work before he had a chance to ask him a few more questions, but when he arrived, Smith's car was already gone.

Josh sat out front and called Smith's cell phone to see where he was, but got no answer. On a hunch, he called Ms. Stapleton.

"Hello," she answered.

"This is Detective Logan."

"Detective, it's very early, what do you want at this hour?"

"Have you seen or heard from Mr. Smith?"

There was a long hesitation. "Well, he called me last night and yelled at me. He called me a liar and a jealous bitch. I don't care if I ever hear from him again. Oh, he told me if I know what's good for me that I'd better keep my damn mouth shut."

"Do you know what time he goes to work?"

"I think he got fired. He told me he was sick of this

town and going to move soon. He couldn't leave soon enough for me.

Josh got out of his car and walked up to the window of the apartment. Nothing looked different. He made his way around to the back. The back door was ajar. He pulled his weapon and cautiously entered the kitchen. "Maitland Police Department, is anyone here?" There was no answer. He entered the living room and then down the hall to Zoe's old room. He opened the door and ducked under the tape and flicked on the light. Everything was the same as when they were there the last time. He pulled the door closed behind him when he exited and crouched as he walked to the other side of the apartment to Jon Smith's room. The door was open. He stepped inside and swung the door the rest of the way making sure no one was behind it. He side stepped to the closet and opened the door. Most of Smith's clothes were gone. Josh put his weapon back into his holster and then pulled open the top drawer of the dresser. It too was empty. He checked every drawer in the room. Everything had been removed. There were still pictures on the walls that looked personal, and the bed was still made. He lifted up the spread and then the sheets. The mattress looked new. The tag was still on the corner of the mattress. It was the same make and brand of the bed that Zoe had purchased. "Could he be that stupid?" Josh slid the mattress up against the wall to reveal the back side. "Well, I'll be damned."

Suddenly, someone bolted into the room and got off a shot, hitting Josh in the chest. He tried reaching for his gun, but the shooter got off another shot. Josh collapsed onto the floor with blood gushing from his back. The shooter ran out of the room, leaving Josh on the floor to die.

Chapter Nineteen

Madison awoke to Sophie jumping up and down on the bed. It wasn't even light outside. "Okay, I get it. You want to go out." Sophie scurried to the French doors. Madison opened the doors and then walked to the kitchen to set the coffee pot to come on in a couple of hours. She was going to try and get a few more hours of sleep before going to the office. Sophie came right back in before Madison had time to fill the pot with water. "Did you even pee?"

She closed the doors, turned off the light and lay back on the bed. She felt restless and couldn't get back to sleep. "Ah heck, I might as well get up. I've been sleeping since yesterday afternoon. I think I'm rested now. She showered, dressed and put down fresh food and water for Sophie. She spread out potty pads in the bathroom in case the investigation took off. She poured a mug to go and started for her car. It was still dark outside, but she was eager to get back on the case. "Oh great, I have no car." She walked down the road to the office and noticed a light on in the back room. *That's strange. Becca always makes sure everything is off and locked.* She reached for her spare key and unlocked the door. There was a coffee mug and files on the table. "Okay, something isn't right, here." She strolled to the other side of the table to see if anything new was on the board when she saw Josh's briefcase on the floor. She picked it up and then dropped it. The hair on the back of her neck stood straight up, and there was a sick knot in the pit of her stomach. "He would never leave this here." She thumbed through the files on the table. She stared at the bank records until she got to the ones about the cash being taken from the account.

Her hands were shaking. She pulled out her cell phone and called Josh. It went directly to his voice mail. She texted him and waited for a moment. The longer she waited, the more anxious she became. She looked at her watch; it was almost 7:00 a.m. She picked up the files again and then suddenly dropped them on the table and ran out the door. Her whole body was shaking, her pulse was throbbing. "Did he go to confront Smith at this hour?" She called Becca.

"Hello, Boss. Are you okay?"

"No, I don't have my car, and I believe something has happened. How soon can you get here?"

"Where are you?"

"I'm at the office. Don't worry about getting dressed for work. Throw on some jeans and shirt and please get here as fast as you can."

Madison hung up before Becca had a chance to ask her what was going on. She grabbed her bag and ran out the front door. She could see Becca's car turn the corner. She ran to meet it. There was no time to waste.

"Madison, what's wrong?"

"We need to get to Zoe's apartment right away. I think Josh went to confront Smith."

Becca hit the gas pedal and sped down the highway. "What makes you think that?"

"He left his briefcase and files on the table, and when I opened the file, I discovered why he wanted to question Smith again."

"What was in it?"

"There were checks that had been written for large amounts of cash after Zoe's death. Hurry Becca, something is wrong; I can feel it."

They raced down the highway to the apartment complex. When they pulled up and saw Josh's car out front, Madison nearly fell to her knees. Becca jumped out of the car too.

"Becca, you stay here."

"I'm not letting you go in there alone."

She followed Madison up to the window, but they couldn't see anything. She ran around to the back and saw the door opened. She cautiously opened the door with Becca close behind her. Madison drew her weapon and entered the apartment. There was no sound, but there was a light on at the end of the hall The closer she got to the room the faster her heart raced. Then she saw him. Josh was lying in a pool of blood.

Out of the corner of her eye, she saw someone darting out of the closet aiming a gun at her head. She swung around and fired one shot between the eyes. The figure crumpled to the floor. Madison kicked the weapon away, checked for a pulse and then hollered. "Becca, call 911." She fell to her knees next to Josh and felt for a pulse. He was barely breathing and was unconscious. "Don't you leave me, Josh, not now." Tears streamed down her face. She tore off her sweater and pressed it against his wound. "Becca, get me a towel." Becca ran to the bathroom and grabbed a towel. Madison pressed that one into the other wound. She felt for his pulse again. She felt nothing.

She heard the sirens coming. "Becca tell them where he is." Within moments, the EMTs were pushing Madison aside and administering CPR. Madison stood at the doorway with Becca's arms around her. "He's strong; he's going to be okay, Maddy."

The Police entered the room to find another shooting victim, but the EMTs told them there was no more they could do for him; he was dead. Madison showed her FBI badge and explained what happened, and then Becca chimed in to give her account of what transpired.

Madison could not stop the tears as she watched them hurry Josh out with a mask over his face and tubes in him. All she could do at that point was follow them to the hospital. They rushed him into the emergency room, but when she tried to follow they stopped her. "You'll have to wait out here, Miss."

"But he's my partner."

"There is nothing you can do now. Let's us do our job."

Madison called the Chief to let him know what happened and then she paced the lobby. After more than five hours, the doctor slowly walked through the double doors. He lowered his mask and reached for Madison's hands.

Epilogue

It had been three months since Josh had been shot, and Madison killed Jon Smith.

The blood stains on Jon Smith's mattress were those of Zoe McClain's, and the mattress was positively identified as belonging to her. It was easier for Smith to use her mattress than try and dispose of it. The police found a suicide note in the drawer next to the bed. It explained he had gone too far, and there was no way back. He was too far in debt. The signatures on the checks were positively those of Jon Smith. Madison deduced the motive was that Zoe had confronted Smith about her money and threatened to turn him in, so he killed her and tried to make it look as though she had just moved.

The Chief told Madison that the shooting was most likely suicide by cop, because he didn't have the guts to shoot himself. She didn't care; the bastard had shot her Josh, and she was glad Smith was gone.

She could finally bring justice for Denise McClain for the murder of her daughter. Madison boxed up all of Zoe's belongings that had been held in evidence and drove out to deliver them to Denise McClain. "Thank you so much for all you did to find my daughter's killer. I'm just so sorry about your partner." Madison thanked her for her kind words. She said her goodbyes and returned to the office.

A few small cases trickled into the office, and with the help of Becca they solved them without any difficulty. News started traveling fast about her agency, and soon calls were coming in, but it wasn't the same without Josh by her side.

Becca began studying for her P.I. license. Madison told her when she got her license she'd be handling cases on her own. But until they found someone to take on Becca's duties, she hoped Becca would continue as her assistant.

The afternoon clouds were rolling in, and Madison knew the sky would open up soon, and the rain would pour. "Becca, why don't we call it a day?"

"Okay. What do you want me to do with all these old files on the McClain case?"

"Just put them in the front, I'll take them over to the Maitland Police Department later.

"I'll see you tomorrow, then. Would you like me to bring some bagels and coffee in the morning?"

Madison turned to Becca. "That would be nice. Have a nice evening."

Madison straightened up her office and then stepped into the case room. She stood there looking at the empty board. "Time goes by so fast. It seems like only yesterday; we were all standing here wiping powder donuts off of Josh. I miss that." She sighed, turned off the light and locked up. She drove home, unlocked the door to a waiting Sophie spinning in circles wanting attention. "What do you want, little girl?" she teased.

"She wants you to take her outside." A voice hollered from the upstairs balcony.

Madison smiled and let Sophie outside to romp in Josh's massive back yard. She poured two glasses of wine and carried them upstairs and opened the doors to the balcony facing the lake.

"You had better get back in your bed Detective. You need to get your ass back to work soon, and you're not going to do it running around up there. She leaned over and placed his face in her hands and kissed him. I need my partner back.

"Yes, ma'am, Agent Hart, yes ma'am.

THE END . . . *for now*

Coming 2016

Another
Madison Hart Mystery: Murder in Maitland

Holding onto Us Trilogy

Willow Trilogy: Willow and the Gift, The Final Chapter

Books by D.B. Jones

Can be found at:
http://www.amazon.com/DB-Jones/e/B00JH298EG
http://www.smashwords.com/profile/view/DBJones
Author

Madison Hart Mysteries
Beyond Secrets
Beneath Secrets

Seasons of Passion Mystery Series
Summer Heat
Nights of Autumn
Storms of Winter

Young Adult Fantasy: The Willow Trilogy
Willow of Endless Waters
Willow and Rise of The Serpent
Coming in 2106
Willow and the Gift

Contact D.B. Jones

dbjones72@hotmail.com

https://www.facebook.com/DBJones.author

https://twitter.com/dbjones72

http://www.dbjones-author.com/

About the Author

DB Jones lives in the hills of Virginia and sits at her desk overlooking the Blue Ridge Mountains where she loves writing Mysteries. Her series are packed with mystery, intrigue, passion, suspense, and murder. She also writes for the young adult and young at heart through her vivid fantasy worlds. She says the diversity challenges her imagination.

Before writing she and her husband composed and recorded melodic flute music for over 30 years until he passed away in 2002.

DB's love of the creative side of life led her to music, painting and then writing. She only anticipated writing the one story that had lain in the back of her mind since childhood. But once she started hammering away at the keyboard, she discovered there were many other characters screaming to have their spotlight on the page.

Her first novel was the beginning of a Fantasy Trilogy, Willow of Endless Waters, but it didn't take long after that until she burst onto the pages of Mystery and Crime Fiction.

DB loves sitting on her patio sipping wine with friends and family and watching her Koi rambling in and out of the many caves and grasses that fill her pond.

Made in the USA
Charleston, SC
04 January 2016